NORBY
THE MIXED-UP ROBOT

JANET & ISAAC
ASIMOV

DOVER PUBLICATIONS, INC.
Mineola, New York

To all who like our robot stories, especially to
H. Read Evans and Robert E. Warnick

Bibliographical Note

This Dover edition, first published in 2009, is an unabridged republication of the work originally published by Walker Publishing Company, Inc., New York, in 1983.

Library of Congress Cataloging-in-Publication Data

Asimov, Janet.
    Norby, the mixed-up robot / Janet and Isaac Asimov.
        p. cm.
    Summary: Jeff Wells, a Space Academy student, and Norby, a second-hand robot with unusual abilities, find themselves involved in the sinister plans of Ing the Ingrate, who intends to take over the universe.
    ISBN-13: 978-0-486-47243-0
    ISBN-10: 0-486-47243-4
    [1. Robots—Fiction. 2. Science fiction.] I. Asimov, Isaac, 1920–1992. II. Title.

PZ7.A836No 2010
[Fic]—dc22

2009028267

Manufactured in the United States by Courier Corporation
47243401
www.doverpublications.com

Contents

1

Into Trouble and Out of School

"Trouble?" asked Jeff, a little shakily. "Why am I in trouble?" He was only fourteen, for all his height, and it seemed to him that he had been asking that question for at least twelve of those years.

At first he had had to ask it of his parents, then his older brother, his teacher, and his computer control. It hadn't been too bad then, but having to ask it now of the head of the Space Command was setting a new record. He didn't exactly feel good about it.

Standing right next to Jeff was Agent Two Gidlow, who was no help at all. He was dressed entirely in gray, and his angry red eyes glared at Jeff with contempt. Even his skin seemed sallow and off-color.

"You're not only *in* trouble," Gidlow said to Jeff. "You *are* trouble." He turned to Admiral Yobo and cut the air horizontally with a sweep of his hand, as if that were Jeff's neck it was passing through. "Admiral, when a troublemaker muddles the computers. . . ."

The admiral stayed calm. The Space Academy, which was under Space Command, had serious problems to face and he was at the cutting edge of it all. The matter of a misbehaving cadet was not something he had to twist his insides over.

Besides, he liked Jeff, who was the kind of tall and clumsy teenager he himself had once been some years ago (though that was beside the point), and he found himself wearied now and then by Gidlow's strenuous disciplinarianism (though that was beside the point, too).

"See here, Gidlow," said Admiral Yobo with a mild frown corrugating his wide, black forehead, "why all the fuss?

Remember that you are not part of the academy and have no authority here. If you're going to follow up every prank by hauling the cadet in question into my office to be grilled by Federation Security Control, I'm going to have no time for anything else. All I've gotten so far is that he was trying to sleep-learn, and there's nothing in the rules against that."

"If you do it right, there isn't, Admiral," said Gidlow. "Doing it wrong is another thing. He tied into the main computer network—he says by accident—"

"Of *course* by accident, Agent Gidlow," said Jeff earnestly. He pushed his curly brown hair out of his eyes and stood as straight as he could so he'd be taller than the agent. "I mean why should I do it on purpose?"

Gidlow smiled unpleasantly. His rather pointed teeth seemed as gray as his clothing and his sallow skin. "If you prefer, Cadet, you did it out of stupidity, which is no better. Admiral, I bring this to you because it is a security expulsion matter, and that's for you to handle."

"Security?"

"The way this cadet tied himself into the main computer network—by accident, he says—has resulted in the kitchen computer getting the wrong set of data."

"Data? What data?"

Gidlow pursed his lips, "It would not be proper to discuss it before a cadet."

"Don't be a fool, Gidlow. If this is an expulsion matter, the young man has a right to know what he's done."

"One thing is—and it may be enough all by itself—as a result of his idiotic link-up, *everything* is being filtered through the kitchen computer. And this means, among other things, that all the recipes are now in Martian Colony Swahili."

The admiral, who had been playing with the buttons on his desk, began to chuckle as he stared into his private viewer. "I see that one Jefferson Wells, age fourteen, failed to pass Martian Colony Swahili last semester."

6

"Yes, sir," said Jeff, trying not to fidget. "I didn't seem to get the hang of it. I'm doing makeup now, sir, and I was trying to sleep-learn before the final exam next week. I'm terribly sorry about the computer. I thought I was following the directions correctly, and I can't think where I went wrong."

"You can't think, period." said Gidlow. "What it amounts to, of course, Admiral, is that until the recipes are reconverted into Terran Basic, or until the kitchen computer is reprogrammed to handle Martian Swahili, there's no way of running the kitchen. No one in Space Command is going to be able to eat. We won't even be able to have canned food released. I think," he added glumly, "we might be able to get a supply of stalk celery that hasn't yet been indexed."

"What!" roared Yobo.

Jeff stirred uneasily. He remembered with a sinking sensation that Admiral Yobo was famous for his thorough knowledge of Martian Swahili, including its colorful expletives—and also for his prodigious appetite.

"Yes, sir," said Gidlow stiffly.

"But that's ridiculous," said Admiral Yobo through clenched teeth. "The computer should *know* Martian."

Gidlow looked sidewise at Jeff, who was trying to stiffen his stand at attention even further. He said, almost in a whisper, "Very important secrets have been shoved into the kitchen computer, along with everything else, and Computer Control now says that everything in the kitchen computer is classified. That means the cook-robots won't work, and it will be a long haul before we can get into the kitchen computer to do anything about it."

"Which means," said the admiral, "it will be a long haul before I—before any of us can get anything to eat."

"Yes, sir, which is why this is expulsion material. In fact, we're going to have to take this cadet mentally apart before we expel him, in order to find out if he's learned any classified material."

"But Mr. Gidlow," said Jeff a little hoarsely, for his mouth had gone dry with fright—he had heard stories about what could happen to people under mental invasion—"I don't know any Swahili, not even now. The sleep-learning didn't do any good, so I didn't get any classified material. I didn't get *anything* except some strange Martian recipes—"

"Strange?" said the admiral, glowering. "You think Martian food is strange?"

"No, sir, that's not what I meant—"

"Admiral," Gidlow said, "he clearly got classified information he thinks are recipes. He *must* be taken apart."

Jeff felt desperate. "There's nothing classified in me. Just recipes. What makes them strange is that they're in Martian Colony Swahili, which I keep telling you I don't understand."

"Then how do you know they're recipes? Eh? Eh? Admiral, this little troublemaker is convicting himself with his own mouth."

"I know the Martian names for some of their dishes," said Jeff. "That's how I know. I like to go to Martian restaurants. My brother used to take me to them all the time. He always says there's nothing like Martian cooking."

"Quite right." Admiral Yobo stopped glowering and nodded. "Quite right. Your brother has good sense."

"That has nothing to do with anything, Admiral," said Gidlow. "The cadet will have to leave school and come with me. I'll find out what he knows."

"I can't leave school," said Jeff. "The semester is almost over, and I've signed up for summer school so I can learn advanced robotics and invent a hyperdrive."

Gidlow sniggered. "With your record, you'll probably use the hyperdrive to send Space Command into the Sun. No one's invented a hyperdrive, and no one ever will. And if anyone ever does, it won't be a numbskull like you. You're not going back to school, because you're suspended—permanently, I hope."

8

Yobo said very quietly, "Am I not the one to make that decision?"

"Yes, Admiral," said Gidlow. "But under the circumstances, you'll find you can't make any other decision. Where matters of security are concerned—"

"Please," Jeff said faintly, "it was all an accident." The dark, paneled walls of the admiral's private office seemed to be closing in on him, and Gidlow seemed to be getting bigger and grayer.

"Accident? Hah! You're a danger to the Solar Federation," said Gidlow. "And even if you weren't, your stay at the academy is over. It so happens, Admiral, that Cadet Jefferson Wells's tuition payments are long overdue. I have investigated the matter and found that there is no money with which to make the payment. The Wells family corporation is bankrupt. Farley Gordon Wells—the so-called Fargo Wells—has seen to that."

"No! That's a l— That's not true!" Jeff shouted in outrage.

Admiral Yobo bent forward in his enormous chair. "Fargo Wells is the head of the family?"

"Yes, sir," said Gidlow. "Do you know him?"

"Only slightly, only slightly," said Yobo without any expression in his face. "He used to be in the fleet."

"Forced to resign—because of general incompetence, I suspect. It clearly runs in the family. And he's just as incompetent in handling the family finances."

"It's not so! It's not so!" Jeff said.

"If it's not incompetence, then it's general sabotage. It's the only alternative. He could be in the pay of Ing's League for Power. One of Ing's spies."

"You're wrong!" shouted Jeff. "My brother is no traitor. He wasn't forced to resign. He *had* to resign when our parents were killed in an accident and there was no one else to run the family shipping business. And I'm sure he did a good job."

"Such a good job," said Gidlow, "that he didn't even leave

9

you enough money to pay your tuition. Which doesn't matter, because even if you had a million credits, you would have to leave—and that should be a consolation to you. You will come with me to Security Control for prolonged probing. And if you know where your brother is, I'll send you to him when we're quite through with you." Gidlow looked up at the admiral. "I tried to locate Fargo Wells and failed."

"I don't know why," said Admiral Yogo calmly. "I've consulted Computer Central, and there seems to have been no trouble." His fingers stabbed quickly at the control buttons on his desk, and the screen on the wall lit up.

Jeff's heart leaped as his older brother's image appeared. He *needed* Fargo's strength and cheer—but that was only an initial feeling, followed by sudden dismay. There was no familiar twinkle in Fargo's sharp blue eyes, and his rumpled black hair was neatly combed.

I really am in trouble, Jeff thought. Even Fargo isn't letting himself be himself on my account.

Fargo's holographic image nodded gravely. "I see that you have company, Admiral, and I can guess the reason. Does our Mr. Gidlow believe that Jeff is in Ing's pay? I admit that my kid brother is big for his age, but no Space Cadet should be forced to undergo one of Gidlow's famous probings. Even the matter of Ing the Ingrate should not justify that."

"Your guesses miss the mark, *Mister* Wells," Gidlow said stiffly. "It is not that we suspect your brother of being in league with Ing—though there are few we can completely trust these sad days. We merely want to find out what classified material he learned from the computer in Martian Swahili, and I assure you we will. You will not stop me, Mr. Wells."

"Gidlow, I admire your firm and absolute assurance, but Space Academy is part of Space Command," said Yobo, "and when probing is in question, I somehow suspect that *I* am the final authority."

"When matters of security are concerned, we cannot have

10

divided responsibility, Admiral. With respect, I make the decisions there."

"With respect, Gidlow, you don't." Yobo rose majestically, looming up like Mons Olympus on his native Mars. "I will decide what's to be done with the boy."

Suddenly Fargo laughed and began to speak in rapid Martian Colony Swahili.

Gidlow gasped, while Admiral Yobo clenched his huge fists and frowned.

Jeff felt bewildered. "Fargo, what are you doing?"

"Mentioning a few state secrets, little brother."

The Admiral looked down at Jeff. "You didn't understand a word of that, did you?"

"No, sir."

"He's lying," Gidlow said.

"I don't think he is," said Yobo. "It would have taken a polished actor to remain blank-faced, considering what Fargo Wells said. It is quite safe to accept the fact that Wells has just proved, in his little charade, that the boy's attempt to sleep-learn failed, as he said it did. He may return to the academy."

"I must protest, Admiral," said Gidlow. "The director of the academy has admitted to me that the boy's tuition is so far overdue that only his excellent—his *previously* excellent—record has kept him in school. She said she thought the boy could get a scholarship, but in view of his damage to the computers, that is not in the range of possibility now."

As Admiral Yobo began to glower again, Fargo Wells intervened smoothly. "There is something in what Gidlow says, Admiral. We don't have much money, and we can't pay any tuition. It's almost summer and my brother can probably use a vacation, and—well, we may be able to begin to restore our fortunes in the interval." He winked at Jeff.

But Jeff drew back at the suggestion. "I don't want a vacation, Admiral. I like it at the academy. I want to join the fleet some day."

"Not this summer," said Fargo flatly. "And it will be worthwhile for you, Jeff. We're not completely penniless. We have a scoutship, and we can get spacer jobs, which will be useful experience. There's even enough to get you back to Earth by transmit so that we can celebrate summer solstice together."

At any other time, Jeff's heart would have bounded at the thought. Summer solstice was tomorrow, and the entire system would be at one in its celebration. All the giant space homes, or "spomes," each with their tens of thousands of inhabitants—the Lunar State, the Martian Colony—all kept the conventions of the calendar of the Earth's Northern Hemisphere. (Even Australia had finally given in.) It was in deference to the original Solar Federation headquarters in the old UN on the Northern Hemisphere island of what was now the Manhattan International Territory, which had agreed to consider itself, rather reluctantly, part of the Solar Federation.

Jeff turned pleadingly to the admiral. "If I can be allowed to stay at the academy, sir, for my summer courses—"

Fargo intervened. "Kids that mix up computers need to get away from them and stay awhile in a nice primitive spot like Manhattan. Under my care, of course. Don't you agree, Admiral?" Fargo and Yobo exchanged a long look.

Jeff felt resentful. He hated it when grown-ups talked over his head as if he were not there. Fargo hardly ever did that. What was the matter?

"Yes," said Yobo. "Go and pack, Jefferson Wells."

"But I—" began Gidlow.

"The boy goes home," said Yobo. "He's of no interest to you."

"Come on, Jeff," said Fargo. "The faster you hurry, the sooner you'll be deprived of Gidlow's fascinating company. Come on, and I'll tell you interesting stories about the misdeeds and ambitions of Ing the Ingrate. Remember the motto TGAF, eh? See you tonight." His image faded out.

"What does that motto mean?" demanded Gidlow.

Jeff thought quickly. "That's just Fargo's way. He means all difficulties can be overcome."

"TGAF? All difficulties can be overcome? Admiral, there is some sort of conspiracy—"

"No," said Jeff. "It's just the way he thinks of difficulties. He's so handsome that . . . well, TGAF means 'the girls are findable.' "

The admiral burst into a loud roar of laughter. "That's authentic Fargo," he said, and Jeff tried to stifle his sigh of relief.

"In any case," said Gidlow, "this boy will not be coming back to the academy. Be sure of that, boy!" He swirled out, the very lines of his back showing his anger.

Why does he hate me so? Jeff wondered.

But Admiral Yobo, looking down kindly at him, said, "Things will be better after a while, Jefferson. I once knew your parents, you know. They were good friends of mine— and good seismologists, too, till Io got them. Not good businesspeople, though, any more than Fargo is." He held out a slip of paper to Jeff.

"What is this, sir?"

"A credit voucher. Use it to buy a teaching robot, one that can tie in to the Solar Educational System. Learn enough to get back into the academy on a scholarship."

Jeff put his hands behind his back. "Sir, I won't be able to pay you back."

"I think you will. I don't think Fargo would ever be able to, but somehow I suspect you have a firmer hold on common sense than he has. Anyway, it isn't that much money, because I'm not all that rich—or all that generous. You'll have to buy a *used* robot. Here, take it! That's an order."

"Yes, sir," said Jeff, saluting automatically. He hurried out, confused and worried. TGAF? Was Fargo right?

13

2
Choosing a Robot

Packing did not take much time. Cadets owned very little besides clothes and notes, although Jeff did have one valuable item, thanks to Fargo—a book. It was a genuine antique, a leather-bound volume with yellow-edged pages that had never been restored. It contained all of Shakespeare's plays in the original, in the very language from which Terran Basic was derived.

Jeff hoped nobody from Security Control would stop him, open the Shakespeare, and see Fargo's underlining in "Henry the Fifth." Or that, if they did, they wouldn't understand the old language.

"The game's afoot," Henry had cried out, but what game was Fargo after with his TGAF? Was it Ing?

Jeff told his closer friends among his classmates about the bankruptcy and the kitchen computer, but he went no farther than that. He put the book into his duffel bag with a fine air of indifference, even though he was alone in his quarters. One should always practice caution.

He took the shuttle to Mars.

Once on Mars, he made a quick meal of spicy eggplant slices on cheese, as only Martian cooks could make it; then he lined up at the Mars City matter transmitter. Through the dome he could see the distant vastness of Mons Olympus, the largest heap of matter on any world occupied by human beings. It made him feel very small.

And very poor.

Maybe I should give the credit voucher to Fargo, Jeff thought. He needs it more than I need a teaching robot. But

I've always wanted a teaching robot, came the immediately rebellious afterthought.

"Wells next!"

For a second, Jeff almost decided to turn on his heel. Why should he take the transmit? It was so expensive.

Matter transmitters had been in use for years, but they still required enormous power and very complex equipment, and the cost of using them reflected that. Most people took the space ferry from Mars to Luna and then to Earth. Why shouldn't Jeff be one of them? Especially now with the family near bankruptcy?

Still, the ferry took over a week, and with the transmit he would be home today. And Fargo clearly wanted him there in a hurry.

All this went through Jeff's head in the time it took for the most momentary of hesitations. He went into the room. It was packed with people, luggage, and freight boxes. The people all looked rich or official, and Jeff slumped in his seat hoping no one would notice him.

As he waited for the power to go on, he wished again that he could invent a hyperdrive. Everyone knew there actually was a thing called hyperspace, because that's what hycoms used for the instantaneous voice and visual communication that was now so common. It was by hycom that Fargo's image had appeared in the admiral's office for instance. That's what "hycom" meant, after all: "hyperspatial communication."

Well then, if they could force radiation through hyperspace, why couldn't they force matter through it? Surely there should be some way of devising a motor that would let a spaceship go through hyperspace, bypassing the speed of light limit that existed in normal space. It probably meant that matter would have to be converted into radiation first, and then the radiation would have to be reconverted into matter. Or else. . . .

Fifty years ago, an antigrav device had been invented, and

15

before then everyone had said *that* was impossible. Now antigravs could be manufactured small enough to fit into a car.

Maybe the two impossibles had a connection. If you used antigravs in connection with matter transmitters (that operated only at sub-light speeds), you could—

He blacked out. One always did that in transmit.

There was no sensation of time passage, but the room was different. It held the same contents, but it was a different room. He could see the clock in the cavernous chamber outside. Not quite ten minutes had passed, so the transmission had been carried through at—he calculated rapidly in his head, allowing for the present positions of Mars and Earth in their orbits—not quite half light-speed.

Jeff adjusted his watch, walked out of the transmitter room, and was on Earth. He wondered if his molecules had survived the transmission properly. Now wasn't this a case of conversion into radiation and back, after a fashion? Surely it could be improved to the point where—oh well!

The matter-transmission people always insisted that it was impossible for molecules to be messed up in transit, and no one had ever claimed damage. Still. . . .

Nothing I can do about it anyway, Jeff decided.

But if you were going to take the risk, he thought, why not do the thing right? Hyperdrive would be much the better deal. It might still mean conversion to radiation and back, but at least you could go *anywhere*, and that would give you much more in return for the risk.

Right now, by transmit, you could only go to another transmit station. If you wanted to go somewhere that didn't have a transmit, you would have to go by ferry or freighter to the nearest transmit, and that could take anywhere from weeks to years. No wonder the Federation was stuck in the Solar System.

And that's why Ing's rebellion was so dangerous.

Jeff called the family apartment from Grand Central Station, Manhattan's public transmit terminal, to let the house-keeping computer have enough time to send cleaning robots out to make a last-minute cleanup of the dust.

The apartment, when he got there, looked as always. Old, of course, but that was as it should be. All the Wellses had been proud to own an apartment on Fifth Avenue in a building that had been kept going, apparently with glue and wishes, for centuries. It had disadvantages, but it was homier.

"Welcome, Master Jeff," said the housekeeper computer from the wall.

"Hi," Jeff grinned. It was nice to be scanned and recognized.

"There is a message for you from your brother Fargo, Master Jeff," said the computer, and a cellostrip pushed out of the message slot with a faint buzz.

It was the address of a used-robot shop, which meant that Fargo and Admiral Yobo had talked again after Jeff had left the office.

Why? Jeff wondered. For old time's sake? Did Gidlow know?

It was still afternoon in Manhattan. There was time to go to the shop.

Jeff felt faintly uneasy about buying the robot now that he was about to make a purchase. Should he argue with Fargo and try to make him take the admiral's money for himself?

But the admiral had to have talked with Fargo on the subject. There had to be something behind all this, but what?

Before leaving, Jeff dialed a hamburger from the kitchen computer, which was always in perfect order, thanks to Fargo. He said, "First things first," and hunger came first, even for him, let alone for a growing boy. (How much more will I grow? thought Jeff.) It was a good hamburger.

The self-important fat little man who ran the used-robot

shop considered the sum Jeff announced he had at his disposal and didn't seem at all impressed. "If you use that for a down payment," he said, "you can have an almost-new model like this. A *very* good buy."

What he referred to as "this" was one of the new, vaguely humanoid cylindrical robots in use as teachers at all the expensive schools. They could tie in to main computer systems in any city and have access to any library or information outlet. They were smooth, calm, respectful, good teachers.

Jeff studied the almost-new model, wishing that manufacturers had not decided years ago to make intelligent robots look only *slightly* like human beings. The theory was that people wouldn't want robots that could be mistaken for real people.

Maybe they were right, but Jeff would much rather have one that could be mistaken for a real person than one that could be mistaken only for a cartoon of a real person.

The almost-new model had a head like a bowling ball, with a sensostrip halfway up like a slipped halo. It was the sensostrip that served as eyes, ears, and so on, keeping the robot in general touch with the universe.

He stepped closer to look at the serial number above the sensostrip. A low one would mean it was fairly old and not as almost-new as the manager of the store made it sound. The number was quite low. What's more, Jeff didn't like the color combination of the sensostrip. Each one was different, for easier differentiation of individual robots, and this one was clashing and unesthetic.

But it didn't matter whether Jeff liked or didn't like any part of that robot. If he used his money for a down payment, where would the rest come from? He just couldn't commit himself to monthly payments for a year or two.

He looked about vaguely at the transparent stasis boxes, each of which held a robot with a brain that was not in operation. Was there something he could afford here? Something he could buy in full? An older model that worked.

He noticed a stasis box in a corner, all but obscured by others in front of it. He wriggled between two boxes and moved one of them in order to look into it. Half-hidden like that, it had to be a not-so-good robot, but that was exactly what he could afford.

Actually, what was inside didn't look like a robot at all. Of course, it had to be one because that was what stasis boxes were for. Any intelligent robot had to be kept in stasis until sold. If the positronic brain were activated and then kept waiting to be sold, it would get addled.

Just standing around doing nothing, thought Jeff, that would addle *me*. "What's in that box?" said Jeff abruptly.

The manager craned his neck to see which box Jeff was referring to, and a look of displeasure crossed his face. "Hasn't that thing been disposed of yet? You don't want that, young man."

"It must be an awfully old robot," said Jeff. The thing in the box looked like a metal barrel about sixty centimeters high, with a metal hat on top of it. It didn't seem to have legs or arms or even a head. Just a barrel and a hat. The hat had a circular brim and a dome on top.

Jeff continued to push the other boxes out of the way. He bent down to see the object more clearly.

It really was a metal barrel, dented and battered, with a label on it. It was an old paper label that was peeling off. It said, "Norb's Nails." Jeff could now distinguish places in the barrel where arms might come out if circular plates were dilated.

"Don't bother with that," said the manager, shaking his head violently. "It's a museum piece, if any museum would take it. It's not for sale."

"But what is it? Is it really a robot?"

"It's a robot all right. One of the very ancient R2 models. There's a story to it if anyone is interested. It was falling apart, and an old spacer bought it, fixed it up—"

"What old spacer?" Jeff had heard stories about the old explorers of the Solar System, the human beings who went off alone to find whatever might be strange or profitable or both. Fargo knew all the stories and complained that independent spacers were getting rare now that Ing's spies were everywhere, and now that Ing's pirates stole from anyone who dared travel to little-known parts of the system without official Federation escort.

"The story is that it was someone named McGillicuddy, but I never met anyone who ever heard of him. Did *you* ever hear of him?"

"No, sir."

"He's supposed to have died half a century ago, and his robot was knocked down to my father at an auction. I inherited him, but I certainly don't want him."

"Why isn't it for sale, then?"

"Because I've tried selling it. It doesn't work right, and it's always returned. I've got to scrap it."

"How much do you want for it, sir?"

The manager looked at him thoughtfully. "Didn't you just hear me tell you that it doesn't work right?"

"Yes, sir. I understand that."

"Would you be willing to sign a paper saying you understand that, and that you cannot return it even if it doesn't work right?"

Jeff felt a cold hand clutching at his chest as he thought of the admiral's money being thrown away, but he *wanted* that robot with its spacer heritage and its odd appearance. Certainly it would be a robot such as no one else had. He said, with teeth that had begun to chatter a bit, "...sure, I'll sign if you take the money I have in full payment and give me a receipt saying 'paid in full.' I also want a certificate of ownership entered into the city computer records."

"Huh!" the manager said. "You're underage."

"I look eighteen. Don't ask to see my papers, and you can say you thought I was of age."

"All right. I'll get the papers filled out."

He turned away, and Jeff squatted. He leaned forward and peered into the stasis box. This McGillicuddy must have put the workings of a robot into an empty barrel used for Norb's Nails.

Jeff looked more closely, putting his face against the dusty plastic and lifting one hand to block off light reflections. He decided that the hat was not all the way down. A band of darkness underneath showed that the robot had been put in stasis with its head not completely inside the barrel.

And there was a strange thin wire stretching from inside the darkness to the side of the stasis box.

"Don't touch that!" shouted the manager, who had happened to look up from his records.

It was too late. Jeff's outstretched finger touched the stasis box.

The manager had hopped over, mopping his forehead with a large handkerchief. "I said don't touch it. Are you all right?"

"Of course," said Jeff, stepping back.

"You didn't get a shock or anything?"

"I didn't feel a thing." But I did feel an emotion, thought Jeff. Awful loneliness. Not mine.

The manager looked at him suspiciously. "I warned you. You can't claim damage or anything like that."

"I don't want to," said Jeff. "What I want is for you to open that stasis box so I can have my robot."

"First you'll sign this paper, which says you're eighteen. I don't want you *ever* bringing it back." He kept grumbling to himself as he put it through the computoprint device that scanned the writing and turned it into neat print in triplicate.

Jeff read the paper rapidly. "You look eighteen," the manager said. "Anyone would say so. Now let me see your identification."

"It will tell you my birthdate."

"Well, cover it with your thumb. I'm not bright and won't

notice you've done that. I just want to check your name and signature." He looked at the signature on the card Jeff presented. "All right," he said, "there's your copy. Now, credit voucher, please."

He looked at it, placed it in his credit slot, and returned it to Jeff, who winced, for it meant that virtually everything the admiral had given him had been transferred, quite permanently, from his account into the store's. It left him with practically nothing.

The manager waddled through the mess of boxes and touched the raised number on the dial box of the one that held the robot in the barrel. The top opened. With that, the thin wire slowly withdrew into the barrel, and the hatlike lid seemed to settle down firmly so that the band of darkness disappeared. The manager didn't seem to notice. He was too busy trying to shift the stasis box into better position.

"Careful! Careful!" said Jeff. "Don't hurt the robot."

With its hat up and its wire out, Jeff wondered if the robot had really been in a position to *think*. He felt again a stab of sympathy. If that had been so, it must have been awful to be trapped inside a box, able to think but unable to get out. How long had it been there? It must have felt so helpless.

"Please," he said to the manager. "You're being too rough. Let me help you lift it out."

"Too rough?" said the manager with a sneer. "Nothing can hurt it. For one thing, it's too far gone."

He looked up at Jeff with an unpleasant expression on his face. "You signed that paper, you know. I told you it doesn't work right, so you can't back out. I don't think you can use it for teaching purposes because it doesn't have the attachments that will allow it to tie into the Education System. It doesn't even talk. It just make sounds that I can't make sense of."

Now, for the first time, something happened inside the barrel. The hatlike lid shot up and hit the shopkeeper in the shoulder as he was leaning over the box.

Underneath the lid was half a face. At least that's what it looked like. There were two big eyes—no! Jeff leaned across and saw that there were also two big eyes at the back—or maybe that was the front.

"Ouch," said the manager. He lifted a fist.

Jeff said, "You'll just hurt yourself if you try to hit it, sir. Besides, it's my robot now, and I'll have the law on you if you damage it."

The robot said in a perfectly clear voice that was a high and almost musical tenor, "That vicious man insulted me. He's been insulting me a *lot*. Every time he mentions me, he insults me. I can speak perfectly well, as you can hear. I can speak better than he can. Just because I have no desire to speak to my inferiors, such as that so-called manager, doesn't mean I can't speak."

The manager kept puffing out his cheeks and seemed to be trying to say something, but nothing came out.

Jeff said, quite reasonably, "That robot can certainly speak better than you can right now."

"What's more," said the robot, "I am a perfectly adequate teaching robot, as I will now demonstrate. What is your name, young man?"

"Jeff Wells."

"And what is it you would care to learn?"

"Swahili. The Martian Colony dialect—uh—sir." It suddenly occurred to Jeff that he ought to show a decent respect to a robot that clearly displayed a certain tendency to irascibility and shortness of temper.

"Good. Take my hand and concentrate. Don't let anything distract you."

The little robot's left—or possibly right—side dilated to a small opening, out of which shot an arm with a swivel elbow and two-way palms, so that it was still impossible to tell which was its front and which its back. Jeff took the hand, which had a pleasantly smooth, but not slippery, metallic texture.

"You will now learn how to say 'Good morning, how are you?' in Martian Swahili," said the robot.

Jeff concentrated. His eyebrows shot up, and he said something that clearly made no sense to the manager.

"That's just gibberish," said the manager, shrugging.

"No, it isn't," said Jeff. "I know a *little* Swahili, and what I said was Martian Swahili for 'Good morning, how are you?'; only this is the first time I ve been able to pronounce it correctly."

"In that case," said the manager hastily, "you can't expect to get a teaching robot that's in working order for a miserable eighty-five credits."

"No, I can't," said Jeff, "but that's what I got it for. I have the paper and you have the money, and that ends it, unless you want me to tell the police you tried to sell an inoperable robot to a fourteen-year-old. I'm sure this robot can act inoperable if I ask him to."

The manager was puffing again.

The robot seemed to be getting taller. In fact, it *was* getting taller. Telescoping legs were pushing out of the bottom of the barrel, with feet that faced in both directions. The robot's eyes were now closer to the level of the little shopkeeper, who was a good head shorter than Jeff.

The robot said, "I would suggest, inferior person, that you return the eighty-five credits to this young man, and let him have me for nothing. An inoperable robot is worth nothing."

The manager shrieked and stepped back, falling over a stasis box containing a set of robot weeders. "That thing is dangerous! It doesn't obey the laws of robotics! It threatened me!" He began to shout. "Help! Help!"

"Don't be silly, mister," Jeff said. "He was just making a suggestion. And you can keep the eighty-five credits. I don't want them."

The manager mopped his brow again. "All right, then. Get it out of here. It's your responsibility. I don't ever want to see that robot again. Or you, either."

Jeff walked out, holding the hand of a barrel that had once contained Norb's nails and had now sprouted two legs, two arms, and half a head.

"You've got a big mouth," said Jeff.

"How can you tell?" said the robot. "I talk through my hat."

"You sure do. What's your name?"

"Well, Mac—that was McGillicuddy—called me Macko, but I didn't like that. Mac and Macko sounds like a hyperwave comedy team. But at least he referred to me as 'he' instead of 'it.' That was something, anyway. It showed respect. What would you like to call me, Jeff?"

Jeff should have corrected the robot. All robots were supposed to put a title before a human name, but it was clear that the robot he had didn't follow customs too well, and Jeff decided he didn't mind that. Besides, he would get tired of being called Master Jeff.

He said, "Have you always been inside a barrel of Norb's Nails?"

"No, only since McGillicuddy found me; that is, since he *repaired* me. He was a genius at robotics, you know." Then, with obvious pride, the robot added, "The barrel is part of me, and I won't wear out. Not ever!"

"Oh, I don't know," said Jeff coolly. "Your label just fell off."

"That's because I don't need a label. This old but serviceable barrel doesn't contain nails any longer. It contains me. I like this barrel. It's good, strong stainless steel."

"All right," said Jeff. "In that case, since this wonderful barrel once held Norb's Nails, why don't I call you Norby?"

The robot blinked and said, "Norby . . . Norby. . .," as though he were rolling the sound round on his tongue and tasting it—except that he didn't have a tongue and probably couldn't taste. Then he said, "I like it. I like it very much."

"Good," said Jeff. And he and Norby walked off, still hand in hand.

3
In Central Park

The housekeeping computer, not having feelings or much intelligence, didn't disapprove of Norby. That relieved Jeff, who realized that he should have known that the housekeeper would not give him anything to worry about, and would, in fact, be incapable of doing so. Of course, the housekeeper didn't *approve* of Norby, either, but that didn't matter.

Now that he was home and could relax, Jeff surveyed his purchase critically. "Does your head come out of the barrel any further, Norby?"

"No. This is all there is of my head. It's all I need. It's all anyone needs. Does it matter?"

Jeff studied Norby's large, oddly expressive eyes. "I guess it doesn't, but how do you get repaired? Do you come out of the barrel?"

"Certainly not. There's no me to come out of the barrel. It's part of me now. Mac welded me in so tightly, this barrel is my armor, my skeleton. Do you get out of your bones when you see the doctor? Come out of the barrel indeed!"

"Don't get mad about it. I'm just asking. How *do* you get repaired? Let's face it, Norby, I can't afford much in the way of maintenance, so I hope you're not planning on breaking down."

"If you're worrying about cost, Jeff, forget it. I will *never* need repairs. I am good at repairing *other* machines, but as you see me, I will always be." Norby whirled rapidly around on two quickly moving feet, but his eyes kept staring firmly at Jeff. Or the front two did—or was it the back two? "As you see, I work perfectly. Mac was a genius."

"McGillicuddy?"

"Of course. Why use five syllables when one will do? Besides, that's what Mac wanted to be called. Mac. I said to him, 'If you want Mac, Mac, Mac you'll get."

"That's three Macs in a row."

"As many as he wanted for the way he worked me out. Of course, he had help."

"Oh? What kind of help?"

Norby, who had been jiggling happily, came to a dead halt. He stared at Jeff solemnly, then sucked in his head.

"I said, what kind of help?"

Norby said nothing.

Jeff said, "Look here, I'm asking a question. You've got to answer. That's an order, and you've got to obey an order."

From under the hat came a small and muffled, "Do I have to? Can't we be partners?"

"Partners! Well, Norby, I see now why your other owners had trouble with you. You spent too much time with an old spacer who was so alone that he forgot you were a robot and treated you like another human being. You're not one, you know. You're my teaching robot, and you're not going to be able to do much teaching if you act insubordinate."

The hat elevated slightly, and Norby's eyes peeked over the rim of the barrel. Only part of them could be seen. "That's not why the other owners had trouble with me. I just didn't want them. I was wrong about them, so I made them take me back."

"Next you'll say you made a mistake with me, and make *me* take you back."

"I might—if you act the way you did just then. And why should you expect me to obey orders? Would you have bought me if I were just another teaching robot?"

Jeff laughed. "If you put it like that, no. I suppose you'd say it was a weird impulse. I think I liked your looks. You're the funniest-looking thing I ever saw."

"Funny? There's a certain dignity about me. Very grace-fully proportioned is what I am."

"All right. Don't get offended again. I guess it was your graceful proportions. It made me buy you on a strange impulse."

"No impulse, either."

"No?"

"No! After the last time I was returned, I managed to keep my head just a little elevated, and I even put out my feeler and grounded it. The manager was entirely too inferior to notice. Anyway, it meant I wasn't going to be sold to just anyone who walked in. I could watch customers and feel them—"

"*Feel* them?"

"Feel their minds. That's why I knew right away that I liked you and—"

"Thank you, Norby."

"Well, you seemed reasonable and not too uppity. You felt like the kind of person who wouldn't come over all superior to a poor robot. I think maybe I was wrong."

"I apologize, Norby."

"All right. Apology accepted. Anyway, I did my best to appeal to you so you would want to buy me, and I tried to get the manager to say nasty things about me—that wasn't hard—because that would get you to want me more. It worked."

"Okay, then, Norby, we're partners." Jeff realized that Norby had not mentioned the loneliness, so Jeff didn't, either. "Could you have fixed that rattletrap taxi we took home from the robot shop?"

"If I had the parts—which would have to be enough to build an entirely new taxi, I think. The taxi's antigrav was so bad we skimmed two feet off the ground most of the way. And the robot brain of the taxi was so old and deteriorated that it should have been scrapped two years ago." Norby sounded distinctly superior.

"Most of the taxis in Manhattan are like that," said Jeff. "Are you going to tell me about Mac and what he did to you and what kind of help he had? I only ask as a friend and partner."

"Oh, sure. No problem. Absolutely. But not now. What I'm going to do right now is plug myself into the house current and enjoy a refreshing electronic bath. I hope you have enough money to pay your electric bill, Jeff."

"So far," said Jeff. "If you don't take baths every hour, that is."

"I am not that gluttonous," said Norby haughtily. He scuttled over to a corner and plugged himself in, his barrel body over the carpet with his legs out just far enough to balance him as he rocked back and forth humming to himself.

Jeff grinned. Whatever this McGillicuddy had done to manufacture Norby, it must have been unique. Jeff had never encountered a robot like Norby, or heard of one either. Wait till Fargo came home and met the thing!

Come to think of it, why wasn't Fargo already home?

Midnight came and went. The summer solstice should be celebrated at dawn. That's what Fargo had said. And he took the celebration seriously, so where was he?

Jeff finally slept, uneasily, because he was worried and because he could hear Norby exploring the apartment, opening books and fiddling with equipment—and he couldn't help wondering if Norby were doing any damage.

But mostly he was worried about Fargo. Fargo was a good brother. He'd been almost like a parent, reliable and responsible, except for his habit of getting into trouble unintentionally and upsetting schedules.

"Wake up! It's almost dawn!"

"Fargo?" said Jeff, rubbing his eyes.

"It's Norby. If you want to celebrate the solstice at dawn in the park, you'd better go."

"But Fargo isn't here, and the park's not all that safe—"

Norby's head popped up to full extent. "Not safe! What are you worrying about? You have me, don't you? I'll protect you."

"You're too little. I need Fargo. He's an expert in martial arts. He's been teaching me, but I'm not as good as he is, and he made me promise I wouldn't go into the park at night without him."

"What are martial arts? Show me."

"All right," said Jeff, getting out of bed and shaking his head woozily, "if you'll let me wash up first."

Fifteen minutes later he was in his pants and shirt. He struck a pose in front of Norby and yelled.

"Well?" said Norby, after waiting a little. "What happens next?"

"You're supposed to attack me."

Norby promptly rushed at Jeff, who leaned back, grabbed one of Norby's arms in passing, and heaved.

The barrel hit the opposite wall and bounced to the floor. All the limbs had been reeled in and all the openings shut as soon as Jeff had let go. The barrel rolled across the room.

"Norby? Are you all right? I didn't mean to throw you so hard. It was just reflex."

No sound came from the barrel.

"Hey, are you damaged, Norby?"

The sound came, muffled and sulky, "I can't be damaged—physically. But my feelings are hurt."

"You're not supposed to have feelings."

"But I do, just the same. Just because you're human doesn't mean you have the right to decide I don't have feelings."

"I'm really sorry. I'll be more careful." Jeff picked up Norby and started toward the door. Norby's barrel was awkward and heavy, and Jeff realized he had a hard task on his hands.

Norby's hat elevated, and his eyes looked at Jeff. "What are you doing, Jeff?"

"I'm carrying you to the park. I thought maybe you wouldn't want to walk on those short legs."

"What you mean is that with your long legs it would be painful for you to shorten your stride to match mine, right?"

"Well, yes."

Norby made a small grinding noise. "You mean well, Jeff, but there's a great deal you don't know."

"I never denied that," said Jeff.

"And well you shouldn't. I'll let you in on a secret."

"What secret?"

"This one," said Norby, extruding a hand that grabbed Jeff's. He then floated upward and forward, pulling a surprised Jeff toward the window.

"You've got antigrav!" shouted Jeff. "Miniaturized anti—"

"Not so loud," said Norby. "We don't need to have everyone hear about it."

"Ouch!" said Jeff, his head grazing the bottom of the lifted windowpane. He had time to be glad that their apartment was so old that it had windows that could open, and then he was sailing across Fifth Avenue toward Central Park. He wasn't dangling downward with an arm being pulled out of its socket, as he would have been if he were holding onto a passive rope. Instead it was as though Norby's antigrav were spread out over him, holding him up, lifting him. . . .

Norby said, "I *thought* I had antigrav, but you can never tell. I suppose I can remember how to work it."

Central Park was beneath them now. Behind them, low in the east, the sky showed a diffuse light behind the skyscrapers even though the sun was not yet up. Beneath them the park was still in the deep shadow of night.

"I've always wondered what personal antigrav would be like," said Jeff, excited and breathless. The wind whipped his curly brown hair back from his forehead.

31

"It's hard work, if you want to know, and I don't know when my next electric bath will come."

"It seems easy to me. Easy and delightful, like swimming in an ocean of water you can't feel, like swooping through—"

"That's because you're not the one who's producing the antigrav field, so it's no work to you," grumbled Norby. "Don't get so stuck up about how it feels that you forget to hang on. Hold more tightly! Also, tell me where I'm supposed to go for this solstice celebration of yours."

"It's in the Ramble—that wooded section beyond the boathouse, with the boating pond circling 'round to the other side. Go down—now."

"Not so fast. I've got to figure out how. We can't just drop. You'll dent a bone or something. Besides, it's dark, and I can't make my internal light bright enough to show the ground without running out of power. I can't do antigrav and bright light both. What do you think I am? A nuclear powerhouse?" Norby circled, and they sank downward, then up again with a jerk.

"Hey," shouted Jeff, "watch out!"

"Look, I've got to get this right, don't I?" said Norby. "It's not easy to ease into the gravitational field and let yourself sink just right." He grunted. "Okay—now—now. I wish I breathed so I could hold my breath."

"I'll hold mine," said Jeff.

"Good! That helps psychologically. It's hard to make out the ground from the shadow in this dark."

With a thump that rattled his teeth, Jeff found himself on his knees and elbows, which were dug well into moist dirt. His head stuck out over a pool of goldfish in the center of the small grassy clearing. They were lucky—it was the very place Jeff would have had Norby aim for if it had been light enough to see.

Jeff could see the goldfish despite the dark. The pool seemed to be lighted from within, which was odd, because

Manhattan was usually too broke for fancy lighting in public parks.

"Norby! Where are you?" Jeff called, trying to shout in a whisper.

The light in the pool brightened, and slowly a shape rose up and out of the water. It was a barrel shape, draped in water lilies. It continued to rise until it was suspended a foot over the water, and then it spun rapidly in the air, scattering drops, as a dog shaking itself would do.

Jeff received some of the spray and shouted, "Hey!"

The barrel slowly stopped spinning. Two legs emerged from the bottom and started a good try at a dignified walk— in the air—down to Jeff.

Norby's hat popped up. "I didn't judge it quite right. I turned on illumination just a little too late. Still, that was an excellent landing, if I do say so myself."

"You'll have to say so yourself," said Jeff, brushing at himself without much effect. "I've got mud all over me, and you've managed to make me good and wet, too."

"You'll dry," said Norby. "The mud will dry, too, and then you can shake it off."

"How about you?" said Jeff. "Are you waterlogged? You won't turn rusty, will you?"

"Nothing damages me," said Norby. "Stainless steel outside; and better than that inside." He carefully untwined a water-lily frond from around his middle and dropped it in the pond with a finicky gesture.

Norby put out his illumination, but it was getting light enough for Jeff to be able to see him even in its absence. "Now I know why a simple judo throw landed you on the dome of your hat," he said.

"You charged before I was ready," Norby said.

"I did no such thing. *You* charged," Jeff said.

"I mean you defended yourself before I was ready."

"No such thing, either. You just can't manage your own

33

technology. You said so yourself when we were antigrav-ving."

"It was hard, I admit, but I managed," Norby said. "Look at that landing."

"You managed imperfectly," Jeff insisted. "That landing nearly drove us through to China."

"Well, I try," said Norby in an aggrieved voice. "You couldn't get any other robot to do this for what you paid for me. Besides, it's not my fault. I was damaged in a spaceship crash, and then Mac fixed me so that I would be undamage-able, you see. He used salvaged equipment for that and—"

"What salvaged equipment?" demanded Jeff.

"Oh, well, if you're going to disbelieve everything I tell you, I've got nothing more to say."

"*What* salvaged equipment? Darn it, you've got to answer my questions *sometimes*. You're a robot, aren't you?"

"Yes, I'm a robot, so why don't you understand I've got to tell the truth?"

Jeff took a deep breath. "You're right. If I sounded incred-ulous, I apologize. What salvaged equipment, Norby?"

"Salvaged equipment from an old spaceship we found on an asteroid."

"That's impossible—I believe you, Norby, I believe you. I know you wouldn't lie, but that's impossible. Nobody's ever found a ship on an asteroid just lying around. Wrecks are always salvaged at once by Space Command. In this comput-erized age, Space Command always knows when a wreck takes place, and exactly where, too."

"Well, this one wasn't salvaged by Space Command. It was just lying there, and it was salvaged by *us*. And how can I tell you which asteroid it was? There are a hundred thousand of them. It was a small asteroid that looked exactly like all the other small asteroids."

"What happened when he repaired you?"

"He just kept chuckling all the time. He seemed very pleased with himself and kept saying, 'Oh boy, oh boy, wait till they see this.' He was a genius, you know. I asked him what it was all about, but he wouldn't tell me. He said he wanted me to be surprised. And then he died, and I never found out."

"Never found out what?"

"About the things I could do. Like antigrav. And how to do it. Sometimes I can't get things sorted out in time, and that's why you could throw me. And then I don't land right because I don't have enough time to make the judgments I need. Please don't tell anyone about this."

"Are you kidding? Of course not."

"The scientists would take me apart, or try to, in order to find out how I do the things I do, and I don't want them to . . . to try to take me apart, I mean. I'd be glad to tell them if I only knew myself."

Jeff sat back, his arms wrapped around his muddy knees. He looked up at the sky, which was reddening now in the onrush of morning. "You know, I'll bet it was an *alien* spaceship. It would be the first real proof that there is alien intelligence out beyond our Solar System. In fact, Norby, if that were so, *you* would be the first real proof of that."

"But you won't tell. You promised." Norby's voice sounded panicky.

"Never! I won't tell—Friend." Jeff reached out and shook Norby's hand. "But we've got to get on with the solstice celebration."

"All right," said Norby, "but that might not be easy. It seems to me that there's a herd of elephants somewhere."

Footsteps were indeed approaching. Lots of them.

Jeff seized Norby and scuttled behind a bush. Down the path between the trees came a group of people. Each person was holding binoculars.

"Bird-watchers," whispered Jeff.

"What are those?" Norby asked. "A new species of human being? I haven't seen anything like that before."

"That's because you spent too much time in space with

McGillicuddy watching asteroids. Human beings like to observe the activities of other animals. These people watch birds, not asteroids."

"You mean they pry into the privacy of birds?"

"Birds don't care."

"But don't these human beings have anything better to do?"

"Watching birds is a good action. Would you rather they stood about and littered?"

"Birds litter. They—"

"Shut up, Norby."

The leading human, an elderly lady in tweeds, stopped beside the fishpond. "Here," she said, "is a good place to watch for owls. We've had them in Central Park for the last century. Before that, they would stop here occasionally, but wouldn't stay. There were always enough rats and mice for them to eat, but either the air was too polluted or the city was too noisy. Either way, they would decide that the price of a good meal was too high. Now they seem to like Manhattan, as all of us good Manhattan patriots do. At least the little screech owls do. I've been told they nest in the trees around here, and since it is not yet sunrise, there's hope we may see an owl on the move."

"I don't want to see an owl on the move," said Norby.

"What's that?" said the tweedy woman sharply. "Who said that? If there's anyone here who doesn't want to see owls, why did you come?"

"I don't like owls. They're probably scary," said Norby.

"Only if you look like a rat," whispered Jeff, "and you don't—though I wouldn't put it past you to act like one. Now keep quiet!"

"There's something behind that bush," said a boy. "Right there!"

"Muggers!" screamed a girl, waving her binoculars. "They'll knock us down and take our binoculars!"

"I don't need your binoculars," said Norby. "I have telescopic vision when I want it."

"Really?" said Jeff, fascinated. "That could be convenient."

"Maybe they're Ing terrorists," said a man, "and they're holding a secret conference here in the park."

The group of bird-watchers was suddenly very still.

Jeff held his breath, and even Norby was quiet for a change.

At that moment, a shape detached itself from a dark tree and swooped down over the heads of the bird-watchers.

"We're being attacked by the terrorists," yelled the same man who had mentioned them before.

The woman in tweeds stood transfixed, clasping her hands. She didn't seem the least bit frightened—only excited. "Look! Look! It's a great gray owl! A Canadian! It's rarely seen this far south! My first Central Park sighting!"

The other bird-watchers paid no attention. They were scrambling back up the path, clutching their binoculars. "Let's go back," one of them shouted. "What's the use of watching birds when terrorists are watching *us*."

Jeff couldn't bear to ruin the bird-watching. He didn't particularly want to get involved, but he had no choice. He stood up, facing the bird-watching leader. "I'm not a terrorist, ma'am, or a mugger, either. I'm here to celebrate the summer solstice. A family tradition."

"Oh my," said the woman. "The owl is gone."

"I hope so," said Norby. "It was big enough to decide I was a mouse."

Jeff pushed Norby with his elbow. "I'd be ashamed to be afraid of a little bird."

"A little bird? Its wings were twelve feet across!"

"Quiet!" said Jeff, and Norby subsided, muttering.

"Perhaps you'll see it again, ma'am," Jeff said.

"I certainly hope so. Seeing it even once was the thrill of my life—but what is that behind the bush?"

"That's—uh—sort of my baby brother. He scares easily."

"I do not," said Norby. "I'm as brave as a spacer."

"As a what?" asked the woman.

"He said he's brave. He's not afraid of anything as long as he knows he can run away."

"I'm as brave as a lion," shouted Norby.

"He's never even seen a lion."

"I've seen lions in pictures," Norby said. "Mac had an old encyclopedia on his ship. I know how to be brave. I don't run from danger."

"Your baby brother talks quite well for someone so small," said the woman, edging toward the bush.

"He's a prodigy," Jeff said, blocking her off, "but he's very shy. You'll embarrass him very much if you come too close. Of course, he does talk a lot, but that's only because he has a big hat—mouth, I mean. Now I really have to start celebrating the solstice."

The woman said timidly, "I don't suppose I could watch?"

"No, you can't. You're supposed to be bird-watching, not me-watching," shouted Norby.

"He means it's just a private family ceremony," Jeff said apologetically. "It's not traditional for anyone to watch."

There came a shout from the woods. "Are you all right, Miss Higgins?"

The woman smiled. "See that. They were very afraid, but they came back to rescue me. That's very touching isn't it?" She raised her voice. "I'm perfectly all right, good friends. I will be right with you." Then, again to Jeff, "Would you like to join our group some other morning?"

"Oh, certainly," said Jeff, "but hadn't you better go back to them? They must be dying with worry for you."

"I'm sure they are. We meet every Wednesday morning and on special occasions. I'll send you a notice. What is your name and address?"

Jeff told her, and she wrote it down in a small black notebook.

Off in the distance, the owl hooted.

"This way!" called Miss Higgins to her group. "We may get another glimpse of it."

She plunged back into the darkness of the wood, and Jeff could hear that she had found her group and was leading them off on another path. Finally the park seemed deserted again, except for the small sounds of animals and the predawn twittering of birds.

"That was horrible!" Norby said.

"Not at all," Jeff said. "It was just a little delay, and a harmless one. Far worse things used to happen in good old Central Park."

"Muggers and terrorists?" Norby asked. "Tell me about them."

"They're violent people from long ago. Central Park is perfectly civilized today."

"Then why did you say you weren't supposed to go into the park at night?"

Jeff blushed. "Fargo worries about me too much. Sometimes he thinks I'm a little kid. Still, the park is civilized now. You'll see."

"I'd better see," said Norby. "I'm a very civilized object, and I prefer to avoid anything uncivilized."

4
Out of Central Park

Jeff stretched. He hadn't had enough sleep, but daylight was on its way, and it was the solstice. "Come on, Norby. Let's go our civilized way to the special place of the Wells brothers."

"Special place? It's yours? You own it?"

"Not really. Not *legally*. It sure feels ours, though. It feels deep-down ours."

"But not legally? If we're going to have trouble with policemen, I don't want to go."

"We won't have trouble with policemen," said Jeff irritably. "What do you think this is? The asteroids? Just follow me." He started to walk down another path on the other side of the fishpond, but stopped and looked back at Norby, who hadn't budged.

Jeff said, "Well then, go on your antigrav if you want to, Norby. I know walking is difficult for you."

"I can walk perfectly well when I want to," Norby said. "I like to walk. I've won walking races. I can walk higher and deeper than anyone; just not faster. Human beings think that fast is everything when it comes to walking, and they're not so fast anyway. Ostriches and kangaroos go on two legs, and they're much faster than human beings. I read about them—"

"In Mac's encyclopedia, I know. Kangaroos don't walk, they hop."

"Human beings hop, and they can't go as fast as kangaroos. Besides, they look undignified when they hop. If they had bodies like barrels, like *mine*, they wouldn't. Watch me when *I* hop."

"Okay, hop if you want to, but watch where—"

It was too late. Norby tripped over a tree root and went over headfirst. His head didn't move downward, however; his legs moved upward. His body rose in the air, upside down, legs waggling out of the upper end, eyes upside down at the lower end.

Jeff tried to be serious about it, and managed for about fifteen seconds. Then he burst out laughing.

"There's nothing to laugh at. I just decided to turn on my antigrav," said Norby, outraged.

"Upside down?"

"I'm just showing you I can do it every which way. It's a poor antigrav that only works rightside up. Anyone can do that. I've won upside-down races. I can be more upside down than anyone else."

"And can you also be rightside up?"

"Certainly, but it's not as dignified, and I wanted to show you the dignified way. Since you insist, however, we'll do it *your* silly way." Norby righted himself with what certainly looked like an effort, then sank down slowly until his feet were on the ground again. He teetered a little, but he said, "Ta *ta*," and stood on one foot as though he were trying to look like a ballet dancer.

"Well," he said, "how do you want me to go? Forward or backward? I can go any possible way. Do you want diagonal?"

"What you really mean," said Jeff, "is that you don't know which way you'll go until you actually try it. Right?"

"Wrong!" said Norby in a loud voice. "And let me tell you one thing, if you're so smart."

"Yes."

In a much milder voice, Norby said, "The one thing I want to tell you is that I think we should walk to your solstice place, Jeff, before the sun comes up on us and it's too late."

He held out his hand. Jeff took it and, hand in hand, the robot and the boy walked on the woodland path into the more deeply wooded part of the Ramble. The sky was sufficiently light now to make it easy to see the shapes of trees and stones.

They walked happily down the path into a deep glade with a little stream running through it, a stream that ran from a spring that seemed to come from a cleft in the enormous rock face at the end. On top of the miniature cliff of the rock face was a railing. There another path crossed the rock, became a tiny bridge, and circled down to join their path.

A willow tree, small but graceful, bent over the stream, and around its roots grew lilies-of-the-valley, their white cups clear in the dim light. The light wind caused them to nod and send out their delicate perfume.

"I like this," whispered Norby. "It's beautiful."

"I didn't know robots could understand beauty," Jeff said.

"Sure. An inflow of nice electricity is beautiful when your potential is down. I thought everyone knew *that*. Besides, I'm not just an ordinary robot," Norby said.

"I can see that. The alien bits in you were from another robot, a wholly different kind, or from an alien computer or something."

"That has nothing to do with it, Jeff. The trouble with you protein creatures is that you think you invented beauty. I can appreciate it, too. I can appreciate anything you can appreciate, and I can do anything you can do. I'm strong and I'm super-brave, and I'm a good companion in adventure. Let's have adventures, and I'll show you. Then you'll be glad you have me."

"I'm sure of it, Norby. Honest."

"Mac always wanted adventures, but he kept waiting, and the result was that he ended up never having any—except finding the alien ship. And then nothing happened."

"Except to you."

"You're right! I got fixed up."

42

"Mixed up, you mean. You're certainly one mixed-up robot."

"Why do you make fun of me? Just to show me that human beings are cruel?"

"I'm not cruel. I'm glad you're mixed up and have the alien parts in you. That's what makes you strong and brave and—"

At that moment Norby, who was standing with his legs stretched to their full length, widened his eyes to their fullest. "Yow!" he yelled.

"What is it?" Jeff asked. He tried to let go of Norby's hand, but the robot held on with painful tightness, while pointing backward with his other hand. Jeff remembered that Norby had eyes in the back of his head.

"Danger!" said Norby. "Enemy! Alien! Death and destruction!"

"Where? Where? What? Who?" Jeff looked here and there and, finally, up, just in time to see motion across the little bridge. Two figures were advancing quickly, too quickly to be made out in the half light.

There were three men; two men chasing one man.

"Norby!" Jeff cried out. "It's Fargo, and he's being attacked!"

5
Spies and Cops

"Let's go," shouted Jeff as Norby lifted them with his anti-grav. "Bombs away!" And they came down directly on the head of the larger of the two attackers. Jeff was ready for the most desperate fight of his life, but the man wasn't. He crumpled to the ground under Jeff's weight, hit his head against the paving, and passed out.

"Get the other one, Fargo," Jeff yelled. He was panting because most of the wind had been knocked out of him.

"I don't have to," Fargo said. He was panting, too. "Your barrel did."

There was Norby, closed up and on his side, next to the other attacker, who seemed to be groaning in his sleep.

"That's no barrel, Fargo," said Jeff, scrambling to his feet. "That's—"

Fargo wasn't paying attention to him. His eyes were shining with excitement. He liked fights and running and risks and danger, while Jeff did not especially like them. He wouldn't avoid them, but he didn't *like* them. In fact, he *would* avoid them if he could, whereas Fargo usually went out of his way to get into trouble. Jeff wondered again, as he often had, whether it was worth being related to Fargo. All in all, though, he always decided it was.

"Now what's this all about, Fargo?" he asked, feeling like the older brother instead of the younger.

"I might ask you the same question. How did you get here? You weren't here a minute ago. Where did you come from? The sky? And how did you knock out that bruiser, and what are you doing carrying a barrel about with you?"

44

"Never mind all that. Who are these guys, and why are they after you? I thought the city administration was going to get rid of the muggers."

"They're not muggers, Jeff. Anyway, not ordinary ones. They've been following me ever since I talked to Admiral Yobo about you and—uh—other things. I thought I'd lost them in the station at Luna City, but that was dumb of me. They just went on ahead and waited at the apartment. Fortunately, I've got this sixth sense. . . ."

"Like me," came Norby's muffled voice. "I've got a sixth sense, too."

"What?" said Fargo. "Did you speak, Jeff? Or is there someone else here?" He looked about.

"Never mind. Go on, tell me. You were coming to the apartment with that famous sixth sense of yours—"

"Yes. Something told me not to go in without questioning the computer outlet I stuck under the doormat, and it told me that the apartment had been broken into and that two men were inside. I questioned it further, and it told me you had gone out before the break-in, so I knew you were safe. Well, there was nothing in the apartment I was worried about except you, and I wasn't going to fall into their trap. I had to find you first. Then we could take care of them together. As we did, kid, right?"

"Don't forget I helped out," said Norby in a loud whisper.

"What?" said Fargo.

"Pay no attention," said Jeff. "So you came to the park?"

"Certainly; I knew you'd be here solsticing. But they came after me, and I had to lose them. I almost did. But just before I got here, there they were when I was practically on you, so to speak, and then you were on *them*."

"Me, too," came the whisper.

"There it is again," said Fargo. "I'm not insane, and I'm not hearing things, and you wouldn't be just sitting there, Jeff, if you didn't know who was talking. You better tell me." He walked over to Norby, still on his side, and looked down at the barrel. "What is this? Don't tell me you brought a libation for the solstice and then spilled it."

"No," said Jeff. "That barrel is my robot."

"Are you kidding? What kind of robot is a barrel?" He put out his foot and pushed it gently.

"That's extremely impolite," Norby said. "Why do you let him do that, Jeff?" The robot extruded his legs and arms and struggled upright. His hat lifted, and two eyes glared furiously at Fargo. "If I kicked *you*," he said, "I'm sure you would object."

"What do you know?" said Fargo, sounding dumbfounded. "It *is* a robot. Where did you get it, Jeff?"

"At a secondhand robot store. You told me to get a teaching robot, and that's what it is. And he's my friend, mostly. Are you all right, Norby?"

"Yes," said Norby, "and I'm glad you think I'm your friend, even though you don't treat me like one. Surely you don't expect me to stay all right when you persist in putting us into these dangerous situations with muggers—"

"That's a teaching robot?" said Fargo.

"He sure is. He's teaching me that life is complicated and dangerous," said Jeff. "But you still haven't told me who these muggers are. Or don't you know?"

"Well, I don't know them by name, but I suppose they're a pair of Ing's henchmen." With his foot he prodded the smaller one, who was still groaning. "They don't seem to be badly damaged, unfortunately."

Suddenly the larger one grunted, opened his eyes, and rolled over, reaching for a short stick that lay in the grass.

Norby extended an arm farther than Jeff knew he could, grabbed the stick, and touched the henchman with it. The henchman yowled and seemed to collapse.

Norby threw the stick to Jeff. "Take it," he cried. "*My* sixth sense tells me you may find it useful."

Fargo walked over, took the stick from Jeff, and examined

it closely. "Hey, what we've got here is an illegal truth wand, with a built-in stunner. That's an expensive item and a beautiful job, too. This shouldn't be available outside the Space Fleet."

"That shows how inefficient the fleet is," Norby said. "Anyone can rifle its stores."

"Don't tell *me* the fleet is—" began Fargo. He broke off and said, "What kind of robot have you got here, Jeff? Robots have a built-in prohibition about harming human beings. It's called the First Law of Robotics."

"There's another sample of gratitude for you," Norby said. "I suppose you would have been happy if that mugger had used the stunner on *you*. You didn't even recognize what it was when it was lying on the grass. Come to think of it, he probably couldn't have managed to stun you with it. If you don't have a brain, there's nothing to stun."

"Listen here," said Fargo, "a robot shouldn't be insulting!" He strode toward the robot, who galloped toward Jeff.

"Leave him alone, Fargo," Jeff said. "He doesn't really hurt human beings."

"Of course not," said Norby. "It's not my fault I fell on one of them. It was Jeff who said 'Bombs away.' And I was just trying to protect human beings—meaning you, Fargo, using the word loosely—by seizing the truth wand before the mugger did. How did I know it was set to the stun intensity? And I didn't mean to touch him *accidentally*. Listen, Jeff, I don't trust that dumb brother of yours. Is he on our side?"

"Yes, he is," said Jeff. "And he's not dumb."

"Well, he worries about my hurting muggers, and he doesn't worry about the fact that he's hurting my feelings, and I call that dumb."

"He doesn't know you yet. And he doesn't know how sensitive your feelings are."

Fargo asked, "Why is your robot talking to you, Jeff, while he's facing me with his eyes closed?"

"His eyes are open on this side," Jeff said. "He has a double-ended head with a pair of eyes on each side. I bought him at the store you recommended."

"Which has a proprietor," said Norby, "who is seriously dishonest—and stupid. He tried to cheat Jeff."

"You mean that the proprietor stuck you with that barrel, Jeff?"

"No," said Jeff. "I insisted on having Norby. He sort of . . . appealed to me. Actually, the proprietor tried to keep me from taking him."

"Really? It appealed to you? And this robot calls *me* dumb?"

"Listen, Fargo. Don't call the robot 'it.' This robot's name is Norby, and he's a very unusual robot. He's just a little mixed up."

"You weren't going to tell anyone about me," wailed Norby.

"Fargo isn't just anyone. He's my brother. He's part of *us.* Besides, saying you're mixed up isn't *telling.* Fargo is going to find that out after he's been with you for five minutes. With you around, it's got to be the worst-kept secret in the world."

"There you go hurting my feelings again," said Norby. "Just because I'm a poor, put-upon robot, you think you can say anything at all to me."

"Let's stop this love feast," Fargo said drily. "We have more important things to do. For instance, our captives are about to wake up. You'd better use the stunner, Jeff."

"We've got to get them to talk, Fargo, and we can't do that if they're stunned. Norby, tie them up before they're completely awake."

"With what?" asked Norby. "I may be a mixed-up robot, but I'm not so mixed up that I can tie up people without rope. Do I look as though I'm carrying rope on my person?"

"Use this," Fargo said, tossing Norby a coiled wire. "This was going to be a fancy solstice celebration in keeping with family tradition, but what with one thing and another, we won't have any at all."

"What has the wire got to do with the solstice?" Jeff asked.

"Never mind," said Fargo loftily. "I'll surprise you next year. That is," he added with a sigh, "if we get to next year—what with one thing and another."

Norby, meanwhile, with surprising efficiency, tied the hands of the captured pursuers tightly behind their backs with the single length of wire so that they were tied to each other as well. He then closed up again and appeared to be just a barrel resting on the grass beside Jeff.

"Give me the wand," said Fargo.

Jeff hesitated. "Don't you think we'd better get the police? Even in Manhattan, civilians are not supposed to take the law into their own hands."

"This is my affair," said Fargo, "and I'll handle the police if it comes to that." He took the wand from his younger brother, who gave it up with obvious reluctance, and waved it in front of the two men. "Welcome to the world, gentlemen. First, your names."

The two men clamped their mouths shut, but at the first touch of the wand, the big, burly one yelped. Then, with a growl, he said, "I'm Fister. That's Sligh."

"Ah," said Fargo. "A sly spy?"

"Spelled S-L-I-G-H," said Sligh. "And you can't keep us, Wells. The longer you do, the worse it will be for you in the end—and for your brother, too. I warn you."

"Warning noted," Fargo said. "But before I cower in terror and let you go, let's find out a few things." He adjusted the wand. "You won't get hurt now unless you lie. Telling the truth pleases a wand like this—and do keep in mind that this is *your* wand I'm using. Any illegality in this respect is on your side." He prodded Sligh. "First, I'd like to know who Ing is, and what he looks like. Is he by any chance a beautiful woman? That might make things a little better."

"I don't know," said Sligh. He was—or had been—neatly

dressed in brown, with slicked-back hair and a long, sharp face.

Fargo continued prodding, but when Sligh didn't flicker an eyelash, Fargo said a little discontentedly, "Odd! You must be telling the truth, unless the wand is malfunctioning. Are you fully determined to tell me the truth, then?"

"Sure," said Sligh, and almost immediately cried out, "Yipe!" and writhed a bit.

"No, I guess the wand is not malfunctioning, so you'd better tell the truth unless you like the sensation you just felt. That goes for you, too, Fister. Very well, then, Sligh, you don't know what Ing looks like. Does that mean you've seen him only in disguise or that you've never seen him at all?"

"No one's ever seen him," said Fister hoarsely.

"Shut up," said Sligh.

"What's Ing's ultimate goal?"

There was a pause, and Sligh's face contorted itself.

"The truth, Sligh Fox," said Fargo. "Even trying to lie hurts when the wand nudges you."

"There is actually no need to lie," said Sligh with a growl. "You know what Ing is after. He wants to head the Solar System—for its own good."

"Of course, for its own good," said Fargo. "I wouldn't think for a moment that he's thinking of *his* own good, or that you're thinking of *your* own good. You're all just a noble bunch of patriots thinking only of others. I suppose you want to replace the more-or-less democratic Federation with a more autocratic type of government."

"A more efficient one with more determined leadership. Yes, it will do Ing good, and me good, too, but it will do everyone good. I'm telling the truth; the wand isn't touching me."

"That just means you *believe* what you say to be the truth. I'll give you credit for kidding yourself into thinking you're noble. Maybe Ing feels that way, too, though I doubt it, and wish I had *him* under the wand. What will you call Ing when he's won out? King Ing? Queen Ing? Boss Ing? Leader? Lord? Emperor?"

"Whatever Ing chooses."

"And how is Ing planning to accomplish all this? Where do I come in?"

Sligh squirmed. "Anyone opposing Ing would have to be negated or converted. You would be an ideal convert."

"You hoped to do it by applying this wand long and hard."

"That would just keep you quiet and cooperative till we took you away. We have other methods for the actual conversion."

"No doubt, but there's more to it," said Fargo. "You weren't after me until quite recently. I wonder why?"

"It would not be advisable for me to tell you."

"I'm sure you believe that, so it's not a lie, is it? Yes, you can avoid pain by telling truths that reveal nothing. On the other hand, perhaps I don't need your revelation. I suspect that Ing's plan is to take over Space Command, first of all. Once that is in his control, he can maneuver easily to take over the Federation itself. And it has recently occurred to him that I would be an ideal person to infiltrate the command and betray Admiral Yobo. After all, the admiral is my friend and trusts me, and I am badly in need of money, and that need will make it easier for me to be converted. In fact, there's your 'other method' for conversion. Plain, old-fashioned bribery. Am I right?"

Sligh hesitated only briefly. "All I can say is that Ing has plenty of money, and he is generous with those he considers his friends."

Jeff broke in suddenly. "Fargo, that's not all—"

"Shut up, Jeff. Now, Mister Sligh, I am turning the truth wand on myself. See, I haven't changed the setting."

"Yes. So what?"

"I'm going to tell you something, and if it isn't the truth, I'll feel what you felt when you tried to lie. Do you think I can hide it? Do you think I'm tougher than you are?"

"No," snarled Sligh.

"Very well. I'm telling you that there is no chance of converting me. I'm out of the fleet and I don't care, because I've got other things to do, but my brother's only ambition is to be in the fleet and serve Space Command someday. He's not like me. He's only fourteen, though he's tall for his age, but he's already shown that he's dead serious and reliable. Nothing will make *him* side with Ing, and nothing will make *me* do anything to spoil his plans. So give up on both of us."

"Is that wand still turned on?" said Sligh.

"Jeff, ask me a question I can lie to."

"Are you interested in women, Fargo?"

"Not at all," said Fargo, who then let out a wild cry and dropped the wand. "Did you have to ask me for that *big* a lie?" he said, holding both sides. His eyes were watering.

Then, as the pain abated, he said to Sligh, "Now let's get back to you and Ing. Tell me—"

Jeff interrupted. "Something's coming."

The soft whirring noise of an antigrav motor sounded not too far away, and in a moment there was a blue-and-white police car hovering overhead. Its searchlight was aimed down at the shaded clearing where the sun, still low on the horizon, had not yet penetrated.

A directed and magnified sound beam came down sharply, its loudness carrying all the overtones of authority: "We are answering a general distress call, giving these coordinates. No one move. We are the police."

Fargo at once stepped away from the two bound figures, dropped the truth wand, and raised his arms. Jeff raised his arms as well. Norby remained a barrel. After a moment's hesitation, Sligh and Fister began to call out, "Help! Help!"

"What in blazes is going on down there?" said the amplified police voice. A figure in blue leaned out, surrounded by the faint glow of a personal shield.

"Hey, Fargo," said Jeff. "Personal shields are finally on the market. Can we afford a couple?"

"Not on your life," said the policeman. "They cost a fortune, and civilians aren't allowed to have them."

"Is that why you don't have one, Sligh?" asked Fargo. "Or is Ing too cheap to get you one?"

"Mine is out of order," said Sligh. "The manufacturer guaranteed it, but—"

Fargo laughed. "I guess Ing tried the bargain basement."

The policeman leaned out further. The personal shield glittered on all sides but did not hide the very efficient stunner that the policeman was holding.

Fargo said, "If it's that expensive, Officer, how come City Hall can afford them?"

"They can't," said the policeman. "Very few of us are equipped with them. Fortunately, for me, the mayor is my father. Now just what is all this?"

"As you can see—" began Fargo.

"Don't tell me what I can see, because I can see what I can see. I see two helpless men tied up, and two others standing near and in possession of what looks like an illegal truth wand. Which in turn makes it look very much like a mugging, and makes me sense, somehow, that I have the honor of speaking to the muggers."

"Hey," said Jeff. "You're not a policeman."

The policeman said sharply, "Do you wish to see my identification?"

"I mean, you're a *woman*."

Fargo said, "Better late than never, Jeff. There's hope for you if, at the tender age of fourteen, you've finally learned to tell the sexes apart."

The policeman said, "A policeman is a policeman, regardless of gender. Now, have you anything to say before I arrest you on the perfectly obvious evidence that—"

"Hey!" said Jeff. "You've got it wrong. We're the *victims*."

"Indeed. Victims are usually the ones that are tied up."

"That's right," called out Fister. "Get us loose. They jumped us when my friend and I were here in the park for a religious observance of the solstice."

"Are you Solarists?" asked the policeman with interest.

"Brought up Solarists by very pious parents," said Sligh. "Both of us. My friend and I. And these two hoodlums violated our religious rights by—"

"Madame Cop," said Fargo. "I suggest you take these two men—and my humble self—to the nearest police station for questioning. Using their truth wand, or a police version if you'd rather, you will soon find out that these men are followers of Ing the Ingrate, and that they were pursuing me in order to force me to join them in their nefarious business. With great skill, I turned the tables on them and—"

"Okay. Stop talking, if you know how. In the first place, untie those two men. When that's done, I will have you grabble-meshed individually to the police car, and my partner and I will loft you to the station. Any objections?"

"I sure haven't," Fargo said. "Jeff, untie those villains, but don't get between them and this stunning woman's stunner."

"Your manner," said the policeman, "is somehow familiar."

"Women usually find it so."

"To an obnoxious extent, I am sure. What's your name?"

"Fargo Wells."

"Farley Gordon Wells, by any chance?"

"That's the full version. Yes."

"You're the kid who put fabric dissolver into the air-conditioning system of Neil Armstrong High School?"

"The same. I *knew* that would never be forgotten. And, jumping Jupiter, you must be the first girl who got it—full-strength. Albany Jones, right? If you weren't wearing that uniform, I'd have recognized you at once, except you probably look even better now."

"You'll never know," said Albany Jones. "And I think my father, the mayor, still has a strong desire to meet you."

Fargo swallowed. "Well, maybe later—when all this is over."

Sligh, who was now standing upright and rubbing his wrists, said, "This is an immoral person, you see. You can't believe anything he says."

"The truth wand will tell us," said Jones. "All four of you take hold of the grabble—"

"Wait," said Fargo. "Not my brother. He's here for the solstice celebration, and he's only fourteen. Please let him go with our keg of nails—that barrel there. You have me."

Jeff said, "Just because I'm fourteen doesn't mean I—"

"Shut up, Jeff. Our parents are dead, Albany. I've had to bring him up, and it's hard being an only parent to a headstrong youth."

"Stop," said Jones, "or I'll dissolve in floods of tears. You'll do; he can go."

"Go home, Jeff," Fargo said. "Sligh and Fister no longer infest the apartment, obviously; but check the door computer first anyway."

As the three men were grabble-meshed upward, Fargo waved and called out, "I'll be back as soon as possible."

Jeff watched them sail out of sight. The park was in full daylight now.

He picked up Norby and tried to balance him on his right shoulder. The barrel seemed to weigh a ton, as though it were full of scrap iron—which, in a way, it was.

"You could at least turn on your antigrav," he whispered into Norby's hat.

Slowly, Jeff began to rise.

"Only a *little* antigrav, idiot!"

Just as slowly, he sank back to the grass, holding what now seemed like an empty barrel.

He began to walk in the direction of home, swinging along briskly, when Norby's eyes suddenly peered out from under his hat. "Are we going home right away? Don't I even get to see the solstice celebration?"

"You can't. We missed it. The sun's well above the horizon."

"Can't we pretend it hasn't come up yet? Who'll know?"

"We'll know. You can't make fun of things like that. . . . Well, I'll tell you what. I can do the Oneness; that doesn't have to be exactly at sunrise. It's supposed to be done each solstice and each equinox. That's four times a year."

"I know elementary astronomy, Jeff!"

Jeff walked back to where they had been interrupted by Fister and Sligh in pursuit of Fargo. It was still in shadow, still fairly cool, and if the brilliance of day was distracting, it at least added a touch of friendliness to the surroundings.

Jeff put Norby down and sat cross-legged on the grass beside the tiny stream. He rested his hands, palms up, on his thighs, and half-closed his eyes.

After a minute, Norby said, "You're not doing anything. What's happening?"

Jeff opened his eyes. He sighed and said, "Don't interrupt me. I'm meditating. I am trying to sense the Oneness of the universe, and you have to quiet your nervous system to be able to do that."

"My nervous system doesn't need quieting."

"How do you know? It's never been quiet. If you don't sit still without making silly sounds, we're going straight home. Just let me tune into the Oneness."

Norby pulled in his arms and legs with an annoyed snap, but he let his eyes peer out from under his head.

Jeff resumed his position. It felt good, as always.

After a while, he said softly, "I am part of the universe, part of its life. I am a Terran creature, from the life that evolved here on Earth. Wherever I go and whatever I do, I will remember Earth. I will respect all life. I will remember that we are all part of the Oneness."

After another silence, Jeff stood up. He bent to pick up

Norby, who extended his legs suddenly and moved away.

"What's the matter?" asked Jeff.

"Does all that apply to me, Jeff?"

"Of course it does. You're as much a part of the Solar System as I am, and everything that lives in it is ultimately of earthly origin."

"But am I alive?"

"You have consciousness, so you must be." Jeff started to smile, but Norby had seemed so serious. "Look, Norby, even if you're not alive in a human sense, you are part of the Oneness."

"What about the part of me that is alien and isn't part of the Solar System?"

"It doesn't matter. The Oneness includes every star in every galaxy, and everything that *isn't* a star or a galaxy, too. Terrans or aliens, *everything* is part of the Oneness. Besides, I sure feel part of you and Fargo and everyone I care about. Don't you feel part of me?"

"I guess I do," said Norby, shooting out his left arm so that he could take Jeff's right hand in his. "Maybe we're *both* important."

He jiggled happily on his backwards and forwards feet for a second and then said, "Jeff, we'd better walk home. That will look better than using antigrav. I feel better. I'm funny-looking, but nobody should mind that. I've got consciousness and I'm alive and I'm at one with the universe. Isn't that right, Jeff?"

"Yes, Norby."

"And what's more, the universe is at one with me, isn't it, Jeff?"

"I think it's more fitting for you to be at one with the universe."

"I think it would be nice to consider the universe's feelings, too, Jeff. I think the universe would be pleased to be at one with me."

"Well . . . maybe."

It was an exceedingly pleasant day. There were joggers moving along the roads now, and Norby waved to each as they passed, crying out, "I am at one with you."

Jeff pulled at his hand. "Don't disturb them, Norby. Jogging is hard work."

"You know," Norby said, "when you were meditating, Jeff, I tried to do the same. I think I had a dream."

"You're not supposed to sleep. Come to think of it, I don't think robots know how to sleep."

"I had to learn while I was in the stasis box. It protected my mind. Anyway, I half-thought I was in a strange land. I was aware of the park, but I was also aware of the strange land. I was aware of both at the same time. Doesn't that make it a dream, Jeff?"

"I don't know, Norby. I don't think that's the way *I* dream."

Norby ignored that. "I dreamed about this strange land that seemed to be something I had never actually seen, but I can't be sure. How do I know where all of me has been, come to think of it? Maybe I was remembering instead of dreaming."

"If you go to this strange land, Norby, don't go there without me."

"I won't go anywhere without you, Jeff, except I think I don't know how to *go* anywhere, really. I only know how to get back."

"Back where?"

"Back *here* from wherever I've been."

"But how can you get back if you don't know how to get there in the first place?"

"I can *go*. I just don't know *how* to go."

"You mean whenever you travel anywhere, it isn't really controlled."

"I guess that's it."

"That's inconvenient, Norby."

"But I'll always get you home. After all, my function is to

protect and teach, so you can't blame me if I'm not perfect at taking you places. You'll keep me, won't you, Jeff, even so? You won't sell me to someone else? I will try to be a good robot."

"I know you'll *try*," Jeff said, but he did wonder just a little bit what good it would do for a robot as mixed up as Norby to try.

6
Manhattan Falls

"Here's Fifth Avenue," Jeff said, rounding the corner of a wall, "and pretty soon we'll be home and ready for a nice breakfast."

"And a plug into the socket for me," said Norby. "Don't forget *my* needs."

They started out across the sidewalk, hand in hand. They had nearly reached the curb when Jeff said in a tense, low voice, "Oh, *no!*"

"What? What?" said Norby.

"Get back!" whispered Jeff, turning and taking sudden, long strides.

Norby went over backwards, and his barrel body made ominous scraping noises on the sidewalk until Jeff shook the robot's arm. "Turn on your antigrav a little!" he whispered.

They melted back into the nearest bush.

"I don't suppose you care to tell me what's happening," Norby said in an aggrieved tone. "I'm just a robot, I suppose. You think I'm just a hunk of steel, I suppose. I don't have any—"

Jeff caught his breath. "Shut up," he said, still panting a little. "Why don't you use your eyes instead of that noisy rattle you call a voice? Can't you see there are men in uniform around the apartment house?"

"Cops?" said Norby.

"Those aren't police uniforms."

"Sanitation men? Park Security? Hotel doormen?"

"Is this a time to be funny? I think they're Ing's men. And

60

if they're strong enough and bold enough to conduct a raid—"

Jeff was talking to himself rather than to Norby, but Norby interrupted. "Maybe they've taken over the city."

"I don't see how they can have done *that*. Manhattan Island runs itself—sort of—and insists on having no outside armed force on its acres, but even so—"

"If it's just a raid," Norby said, "they're taking a big chance and they have to be after something important. I guess they must be after me."

"*You?*"

"Who else? It's our apartment house, isn't it? And you and I live there, and we've just had a fight with two of Ing's men and it can't be *you* they're after, so it's got to be me. That's logic. I'm very good at logic."

"Why does it have to be you? Why can't it be me?"

Norby made a sound like a snort and didn't answer. "They can't have taken the whole city," he said. "Albany Jones approaches."

A police hover-car was circling above, moving slowly as though searching for something. The uniformed men guarding the entrance to the building shot at the car without effect.

"How do you know it's Albany?" Jeff asked.

"It's her car. I don't know if she's in it, of course, but it's her car. I tune into motors. It's very simple to recognize one from another. That's one of the things I could teach you besides languages. Don't forget I'm a teaching robot. Languages are my specialty, but I'm sure I could manage a few other things."

The hovering police car dropped a spine-cluster into the midst of the men below. Understandably, the result was panic. Some of the men dived for the doorway and the others for the two ends of the block. When a spine-cluster explodes, the results are felt only in the immediate vicinity and are not fatal, but those at the receiving end feel as if they've tangled with twenty porcupines. And removing the spines is neither easy nor painless.

Street traffic diverted quickly as drivers recognized that a fight was going on.

"Why don't you signal the hover-car?" Norby said. "It has to know where we are."

"I was about to," said Jeff, waving energetically from behind the bush. The police car sank downward slightly, and something fell out. Jeff tried to catch it, misjudged, and received it roughly on his right shoulder.

"Ouch!" he groaned. "Ever since I met you, Norby, things have been falling on me, or I have been falling on things. I feel black and blue all over. Why didn't *you* catch it? You can't be hurt."

"My feelings can. And with you lurching around trying to catch it, what could I do? You nearly stepped on me as it was."

Jeff was still rubbing his shoulder. "What is this?"

"It's the same belt device that Albany was wearing in Central Park—a personal shield. If you use it, Ing's men won't be able to touch you."

"But how am I going to use it? I don't know how it works."

"That's why you have *me*. I know how it works. I've already deciphered its simple mechanism. Put it on, then turn this switch here when you need protection. Your arms go in these places. No, no, that metal part goes in front. Can't you see?"

"That metal part," grumbled Jeff, "is what hit my shoulder. Is it on right now?"

"Yes," said Norby, "though actually I'm plenty of protection for you anytime."

"Anytime there's no danger." Jeff turned the switch on the belt and was instantly aware of the faint radiance that surrounded him. The street, the sky, and the buildings all took on a slightly yellow tinge that made everything look particularly bright and cheerful.

Norby didn't sound cheerful, however. "Jeff! I can't get through to you."

"Sure you can, Norby. I hear you perfectly."

"I don't mean that. I mean I'm outside the field."

Jeff turned off the field, picked up Norby, and turned the field back on. The personal shield enveloped them both.

"What's the difference?" Jeff said. "You can't be hurt, and if you can protect me, you can surely protect yourself."

"I get lonely," said Norby.

The police car had descended nearly to surface level. Albany leaned out and shouted, "Get in! Hurry! Those Ingrates are coming up with a full-sized blaster."

Jeff tried to climb aboard with Norby desperately hanging onto him. Norby activated his antigrav and it came on so strongly that Jeff found himself turning upside down. Albany pulled him in. "Goodness," she said, "you and that barrel are light. Don't you have any insides?"

Jeff could hear shouting and heavy footsteps behind him. There was the sound of an unpleasant explosion as the car zoomed upward. It shook in the air vibrations but remained untouched.

"Ing's men seized the police station," Albany said. "They came right behind me. They may have seized all the police stations in Manhattan." She bit her lip and shook her head. "I'm afraid we've underestimated the Ingrates. They always seemed a minor nuisance, a bunch of inept terrorists. But it's clear now that that was just a screen. They've set up a formidable force, and they're prepared to take over the system."

"How did you get away?" Jeff asked anxiously.

"My personal shield, of course. I must tell my father to get the City Council to equip *all* the cops with shields. But I suppose it's too late now, at least for Manhattan. It's Space Command that—"

"But what about Fargo?" Jeff said anxiously.

Albany swallowed. Her brows contracted unhappily over

her large eyes. "The truth is I don't know. They grabbed him when they came out of the police transmit, and I was so busy getting away I had no chance to see what became of him. He had given me his address when I was taking him to the station." She looked a little guilty. "We always get the names and addresses of those we take into custody," she added. "Purely routine."

"Yes, yes," said Jeff, who wanted her to get to the point. What had happened to Fargo?

"I drifted by the apartment house, just in case he had gotten away and gone there. I had no idea where else he might go. When I saw the house guarded by the Ingrates, I thought he might have been trapped in the vicinity. Then, of course, I found *you*." She said that with a certain note of disappointment.

Jeff disregarded that. "Then you don't know where Fargo is?"

"No. I'm afraid I don't. What we've got to do now is to find a transmit in Manhattan that hasn't been taken over by the Ingrates. We've *got* to notify Space Comand, or the Ingrates may be able to take over all Earth. They wouldn't attack Manhattan unless they've already seized the key communications network. That's what worries me." She paused and looked solemnly at Jeff. "If we can't notify Space Command—"

"Put me down, Miss Jones," Jeff demanded. "I have to find Fargo!"

"I can't put you down. You'd be taken instantly. And there's no need to worry about Fargo. Your brother is quite attractive. . . . What I mean is, he's quite intelligent, and I'm sure he can take care of himself. We have bigger worries. Space Command itself may be infected by Ing's people."

"Fargo had some kind of private conversation with Admiral Yobo," Jeff said. "That may have been the problem they were concerned with. And maybe *that's* why Fister and Sligh were after him. They didn't want to convert him. They wanted to finish him. Miss Jones, *please* let me look for him. They'll kill him."

"If I may make a suggestion," Norby said.

Albany jumped at his voice, and the hover-car lurched as she inadvertently yanked at the controls. "That's not a barrel," she said. "It's a robot. Don't let that silly thing get in our way."

"That silly thing!" shouted Norby. *"You're* the silly thing, or you wouldn't be so busy talking you can't see the danger right ahead. There are cars approaching, shield-protected hover-cars that probably belong to this Ing person you're so worried about. If I were you, I'd go somewhere else quickly, but, of course, I'm just a silly thing, so don't listen to me."

"Ing's cars?" Albany looked about in horror. It was clear that the trouble was even worse than Norby had thought. They were surrounded.

Albany's mouth tightened. "Ing must have been planning this a long time. He's taking over Manhattan as though it were a meatball and he were a wolf. Well, we've got shields. Shall we fight it out?"

"With what?" said Jeff.

"I've got a long-range stun gun and a hand-blaster."

"Will they work on shielded cars?"

"No," admitted Albany.

"Does this car have shielding?"

"Are you kidding? With the Manhattan fiscal situation? No, only our personal shields, courtesy of Daddy."

"Then they'll destroy our hover-car in fifteen seconds, and we fall"—Jeff looked down for a quick estimate—"thirty stories, I think."

"You might as well surrender, then," Norby said. "That will give us time, and I'll be able to think of some way of saving the situation. I'm terribly ingenious."

"Is surrendering a sample of your ingenuity?" Albany asked. "Anyone can surrender—"

"There's nothing else to do right now," Jeff said, "and it

may be the only way of finding Fargo. We'd better do it right away. One of Ing's cars looks as though it's bringing a blaster to bear on us." He turned off his shield and handed the device to Norby. "Can you hide this in your—uh—inside?"

"I suppose I can," Norby said, "but it will make me feel as though I have indigestion. Why don't *you* swallow it? You have a sort of hollow inside, too."

"Funny, funny. Here, take Miss Jones's."

Carefully, while making little noises of displeasure, Norby put away both shield devices as Albany took the hover-car down to the ground. They were followed, of course, and when the Ingrates swarmed out of their cars, Albany and Jeff surrendered.

They were careful to look scornful and superior when they gave themselves up. At least they tried, and it was especially hard for Jeff, who kept Norby under his arm. Norby made no attempt to look either scornful or superior. He merely concentrated on looking like a barrel.

The Central Park Precinct Station was inside an old brick building and had the aura of centuries of use and occasional slipshod repairs.

Sligh and Fister hustled Albany and Jeff toward the station's transmit. Despite the chronic shortage of municipal funds and the best efforts of every city councilman, there seemed no way of economizing on those transmits. Each police station simply had to have one for any necessary travel through space.

Jeff was still holding Norby. Sligh scowled. "You're not dragging that barrel around everywhere, Wells," he growled. "It made a lump on my head once, and you're not going to use it as a weapon again. Hand it over and I'll melt it down for scrap. Or we'll use it as ballast. Maybe we'll just smash it with a sledgehammer."

Jeff clutched Norby tightly. "I need this barrel," he said. "It's a device that's necessary to—to my health."

"Are you going to tell me you've hidden a kidney filter in that old barrel?"

"I didn't *want* to tell you."

"And I suppose you'll die without it?"

"I, ah. . . ." Jeff hated to lie, but Sligh seemed to be doing it for him.

"You're not fooling me, you dumb kid," said Sligh. "You look too big and healthy to need any machine for your health. I bet that's got Wells money in it. Maybe gold. Give it over!"

Norby whispered through his hat, "Don't stand there, Jeff. Step back into the transmit."

Jeff paused to wonder what Norby had in mind, and suddenly he felt a pinch.

"Hurry up!"

Albany was already in the transmit. Fister and Sligh, facing it, were on either side of Jeff, who had his back to it. The pinch made Jeff jump backwards, and as he did, Norby's hands extended full length, pushing Fister and Sligh in the other direction, out of the transmit doorway.

Albany, reacting at once, slammed the door shut. "Now what? The transmit mechanism works from outside."

"Maybe so," said Norby, leaning against the door, "but I'm managing to work it through the metal—didn't I tell you I'm ingenious?"

"They're going to force their way in—" began Albany.

"I'm almost finished," Norby said.

"But we have to get to where they've taken Fargo," Jeff said.

"I'm sensing his presence," Norby said, "and I'm adjusting the controls so we'll go there directly. I hope."

A queasy sensation hit Jeff in the pit of his stomach, and he blacked out dizzily. When he came to, he saw that they were in a different transmit. He scrambled to his feet and helped Albany to hers. She brushed at her clothing and seemed pretty annoyed.

"You didn't exactly handle that in a smooth way, Norby," Jeff said.

"Well," said Albany, "I don't suppose we can blame your robot. The transmit is old and not working well. I don't think any of the city transmits have had repairs for five years."

"Norby, are you going to be able to get the doors open?" Jeff asked.

"In a minute. In a minute. And—on the other side—we will find your brother." The doors opened, and they stepped out into a huge, gray room. Overhead there was a section of glassite dome and beyond that a dim, rolling fog.

"Or maybe we won't," Norby said in a small voice.

"Where on earth—" said Albany.

"I don't think *anywhere* on Earth," said Jeff. "Norby! Where are we?"

"Is there a city named Titan anywhere on Earth?" Norby asked.

"A city named what?"

Norby pointed to a cabinet to one side with a sign on it in old Gothic print that was hard to read.

Jeff said blankly, "What does it say?"

"It's in Colonial German. That's another language I can teach you. It would come in handy anywhere beyond the asteroids."

"*Beyond the asteroids?*" said Jeff in a shout. "What does it *say*? I don't care if it's Sanskrit. What does it say?"

"It says 'Property of Titan outpost.' I figure Titan is a city in the German sector of the European Region and I just may have miscalculated a small bit."

"Titan," said Jeff in an exasperated tone, "is a satellite of Saturn, and you have miscalculated *a whole lot.*"

"Are you sure?" Norby asked. "It could happen to anyone."

"Of course I'm sure. Where on Earth would we be under a dome? Look up there. You realize Titan has a thick atmosphere that is mostly nitrogen at a temperature near its liquefying point. You might have gotten us *outside* the dome, and then Miss Jones and I would have died a horrible death."

"How could I have gotten you outside the dome?" Norby shouted. "I sensed human beings, and I thought it was Fargo. There are no human beings outside the Titan dome, so I wouldn't have brought you there. There are human beings *inside* the dome, and it's not my fault one of them isn't Fargo."

He turned back to the transmit controls. Jeff blacked out again.

"We're here!" said Albany. "Space Command! Thank goodness! We're safe. Norby, you rate a medal."

"No, he doesn't," said Jeff angrily. "He rates a blaster shot in the bottom of his barrel. Those are not Space Command uniforms."

"Are you sure?" said Albany.

"Well, look at them again."

Two men approached them as if ready to attack. "Down with the enemies of Ing the Incomparable!" they shouted as they rushed at them.

"Oh, *no*," said Albany. "They've even taken over out here."

One of the men reached Albany, but seemed to trip and went flying over her shoulder.

She looked pleased. "Did you see that?" she asked. "It works. They taught me judo and combat techniques during training, but I didn't think I could really—oof—"

The other man reached her and threw an arm about her neck.

Jeff rushed toward her. In a strangled voice, Albany said, "No, let me handle him. Get the other one."

The first man was getting groggily to his feet. Jeff stepped back to let him rise, but Norby kicked him in his rear end and he went down on his face. Norby then rose in the air, turned off his antigrav, and came down hard on the back of the Ingrate, knocking his breath completely out of him.

Albany, meanwhile, was swaying back and forth with the second Ingrate, who was trying to tighten his grip on her. In rapid succession, she dug her elbow into his solar plexus with a hard jab and stomped fiercely on his toes with her heavy police boot while smashing into his nose with the back of her head. He let out a screech and let go. Albany seized his wrist, spun on her toe, and twisted his arm. When he bent, she placed her hip under him, twisted harder, and sent him flying. He hit his shoulder hard when he landed and lay groaning.

"Let's get into the transmit before any others come," Albany said.

As soon as they were safely inside the transmit with the door closed, Norby extruded from within his barrel body a thin, flat metallic tape that spread out horizontally. He pressed the tape against the wall.

"Ah," he said, "I should have done this the first time. It greatly intensifies my sensitivity and my powers of concentration. It takes a great deal out of me, however, and I never know when I'll get my next gulp of electricity. If ever."

"Have you got Fargo this time?" asked Jeff anxiously.

"Yes. Definitely. No mistake."

Again Jeff felt that queasy sensation, but he managed to retain consciousness this time.

"This transmit is in better condition," Norby said. "And now I think we'll find Fargo."

The doors opened, and Norby said, "In fact, I'm sure you'll find Fargo, because there he is!"

Jeff could see an enormous room draped with banners and lined on either side with armed men. In the center was a platform, upon which rested what could only be a throne. Fargo, his arms folded across his chest, was sitting on the

70

edge of the platform, and someone else—someone clothed in metal to such an extent that he looked very nearly a robot—sat on the throne.

"Here's company, anyway," Fargo said. "The beautiful Albany Jones, my resourceful brother, and his graceful barrel. How did you find me anyway? And why haven't you brought an army with you?"

"Silence!" roared the figure on the throne in a voice as metallic and rasping as a defective machine.

"Ing speaks!" said Fargo sarcastically. "Let all be silence, while I welcome the newcomers to the court of Ing the Innocent. Note the distortion of his voice, which is un-euphonious even when undistorted. Note the graceful aluminum of his costume, designed to cover an unattractive body, and the facial mask which serves to spare his audience a view of his face, which is deformed, or his feelings, which are disgraceful, and the—"

The man on the throne gestured, and a guard stepped up to Fargo and lifted a weapon threateningly.

"Since Ing fears words but is brave enough to attack an enemy when the odds are a hundred to one, I shall be quiet," said Fargo.

Albany and Jeff marched up to Fargo, Jeff holding Norby—who was, of course, tightly shut.

Ing's voice sounded again, harsh and repugnant. "We have here two brothers who, between them, know a great deal about the Space Academy and the fleet. And what they know, I will know!" His voice took on the sound of contempt. "In addition," he rasped, "we have a lady cop with a rich father who will help me take over Earth, if he wants his little girl back in her present shape and form. And I see something that looks like a barrel. Give it to me, Jeff Wells."

Jeff held Norby tighter and said nothing.

"It won't do you any good to hold it," said Ing. "I am told it is a curious barrel with arms—when it wishes to have arms. And legs, too. It is something I wish to examine. Hand it over, boy, or I'll have it separated from you at your shoulders."

Norby whispered through his hat, "Move closer to Miss Jones."

Jeff cautiously stepped sideways until his elbow was against Albany's shoulder.

"Now both of us move toward Fargo," Norby whispered. "We've all got to be touching."

"I'll touch Fargo," whispered Albany. "But why?"

"I have an ingenious idea," said Norby in his ordinary voice.

"It talks!" said Ing. "It is a robot and I want it. I am emperor here, and I must be obeyed."

"The history of emperors on Earth has been a sad one," Fargo said. (Albany was leaning against Fargo's shoulder, and Jeff against Albany's.) "Let me tell you about Napoleon Bon—"

"Keep quiet!" Ing barked. "Sergeant! Get me that robot. Kill the woman if any of them resist!"

Norby suddenly cried out. "The personal shields!" He tossed one to Albany and one to Fargo. Then he clung tightly to Jeff and hummed a strange sound.

7

Hyperspace

"Comet tails!" said Norby.

"Where are we?" Jeff asked as he stared at the strange castle on the hill facing them. Terraced gardens spilled down the hill, and directly ahead was an elegant marble castle in miniature.

"What I did," Norby said hurriedly, "was to transfer Fargo and Albany outside the building. That would give them a head start. With their personal shields and Albany's knowledge of judo and Fargo's quick wit—you're always telling me how bright he is—they ought to rally a counterattack—"

"Yes, yes," said Jeff impatiently, "but where are *we?*"

"Well," said Norby, his hat swiveling as he looked about, "what I was trying to do was to get us to Space Command. I memorized the coordinates Mac gave me long ago, but maybe they weren't right."

"Yes, yes," said Jeff, still more impatiently. "Where *are* we?"

"Well," said Norby, "that's the one little thing I don't know."

"You don't know!" Jeff looked about, despairing. The surroundings were beautiful. The sunlight was bright and warm. There was a soothing rustle all about, but where on Earth—or off Earth—were they? "Can't you do *anything* right, Norby? You're a poor excuse for a robot."

"I *try*. It isn't always easy." Then Norby said in a small voice, "I wanted you to own me. I see now that it was a great wrong. You're all mixed up with a robot that's all mixed up.

73

I'll try to get you home, Jeff, and I'll stay here, and you'll be rid of me. I'm sorry."

"No," Jeff said. "I don't *ever* want to be rid of you. It doesn't matter how mixed up you are; I'll just be mixed up along with you." He reached for Norby. "I wish you weren't so hard," he said. "It's difficult to hug you."

"I don't care," said Norby. "Hug me anyway. I'm so glad you want to keep me."

"Just the same," said Jeff, "I wish we knew where we were."

At that moment something came out of the small castle. It looked distinctly dinosaurish, except for its size.

"A miniature allosaurus?" said Jeff uncertainly. He stepped back.

The creature came up to his knee; it wasn't even as tall as Norby. It was wearing what seemed to be a gold collar and, as it swished its tail, it emitted a series of variegated sounds.

"Is it talking or just making noises?" Jeff asked, feeling an extreme urge to reach out and pat its reptilian head.

"Don't you understand it?" Norby asked. "I keep forgetting that you're not a linguist. It—or rather, she—says you're cute."

"I think she's cute, too, but what's a miniature dinosaur doing anywhere on Earth? And how is it that she talks?"

"I don't think this is Earth," Norby said.

"But you understand the language. Doesn't that mean you ought to know where this is?"

"To tell the truth, Jeff, I don't know how I come to understand the language. I didn't know it was in my memory banks until I heard it. And I don't remember ever having been here before—unless—unless this is the place I dreamed about."

"But what did you do to get here?" Jeff was scarcely aware that the dinosaur was nuzzling his hand. Automatically, he began stroking her head.

"I just shifted through hyperspace. That's why it's so hard

to get back. I could always get you back through normal space, but. . . ."

"You went through hyperspace without a transmit?" asked Jeff in a half-shout.

Norby retreated a step. "Is that illegal?"

"It's impossible. No one can do it."

"I did it."

"But that's true hyperspatial travel. How did you come to know how to do that?"

"I thought everyone knew how."

"Well, then, how do you do it?"

Norby thought awhile. Then he said, "I know *how* to do it, but I don't *know* how to do it."

"That doesn't make sense." Jeff was sitting on the grass, and the creature had her forepaws in his lap and her head resting on his shoulder. She was making a sound like a soft "Gruffle, gruffle, gruffle." Jeff was running his hand down her long neck, which had pointed projections all the way to the tip of her tail.

"Do you know how to raise your arm?" Norby asked.

"Certainly."

"Do you *know* how to raise it? Can you explain exactly what it is you do to raise your arm? What happens inside your arm that makes it go up?"

"I just decide to have my arm go up, and it does."

"Well, I just decide to jump through hyperspace, and I just do. I can go anywhere in an instant. But I don't *know* how I do it."

"But, Norby, that makes you the most valuable creature in the Solar System—"

"Oh, I know that."

"I mean, you *really* are. No one else knows how to go through hyperspace without transmits. It would be the greatest discovery of the age if any human being could make it." Jeff began stroking the dinosaur faster and faster. "It was my ambition to make the discovery myself. That's why I

75

wanted to go through the academy and learn all I could about hyperspatial theory. It's my dream to invent hypertravel some day. Now, with you to help me—"

"I said I only know *how* to do it, nothing else. Is that why you want to be with me, Jeff? Because I know how to hypertravel?"

"*No.* I told you I was glad I was with you *before* you told me about it. But now I'm twice as glad." Jeff was pulling the creature toward himself, yet he still wasn't aware of it. "Well then, if you came here, where are we?"

"But that's the other thing, Jeff. I know how to do it, but I guess I don't know how to aim right. I intended to go to Space Command, and I miscalculated. I don't know where we are—and yet I know that creature's language."

Jeff looked down at the dinosaur and suddenly realized that she was softly licking his left ear with her warm, dry tongue. He went over backward, and she tumbled out of his lap. She got to her feet and unfurled the leathery ridges on each side of her back spines.

"Wings!" Jeff choked. "She's got wings! She's a pterodactyl or something."

"Nonsense," said Norby. "Any fool can see that she's a dragon."

"Dragons are mythical beasts."

"Not here."

"What makes you so sure? You don't even know where 'here' is."

"I think part of me knows, but I can't tune in to it. I'm sorry, Jeff. I'm so mixed up, I think I ought to be destroyed."

"Not before you get us back. And even then, I won't let anyone destroy you. But get us back, Norby. It's important."

"Don't get mad, Jeff, but I'm having a little trouble figuring out how. I may have moved far out of the Terran Solar System. If only I could remember where this was! Part of me seems to have been here before, or why would I dream of it?"

76

"You know . . . I'll bet it's the alien mechanisms McGilli-cuddy used in you. The alien thing, whatever it was, was once here, whenever *that* was, and you just snapped back to that place without really thinking."

"In that case—Hey!" Norby went over sideways as the little dragon broke into a sudden run and pushed past him. She ran into the small castle.

Jeff helped Norby up.

"Baby dragons *never* have manners," Norby said. "I remember when—" He paused. Then in a discouraged voice he said, "No, I don't remember. For a minute, I was sure I had remembered remembering dragons, but I don't."

"You're getting me confused again."

"I can't help it. Maybe we'll be stuck here too long to be able to help Fargo and Albany defeat Ing."

"I'm hungry, Norby. Maybe we can find some forms of life to eat. But what about you? You'll never be able to plug into an electric socket here. You'll starve. Maybe *that* will inspire you to remember how to get back."

"Actually, I can't starve. Electric sockets give me between-meal snacks. For the real thing I dip into hyperspace, and I can do that anywhere, anytime. There's unlimited energy in hyperspace. You ought to try it."

"I would, if I were able to," Jeff said. "What's hyperspace like?"

"It's nothing."

"That's very helpful."

"I mean it. Hyperspace is nothingness. It isn't space or time, so it has no up or down or when or where. When I'm in it, I can sense a . . . well, sort of . . . I guess it's a pattern that isn't really there but is potentially there because that's what the actual universe is, the pattern that's sort of potentially there in hyperspace. . . ."

"Norby!"

"Well, I didn't say I could explain it. I can't. All I know is that hyperspace is definitely potential—I mean, it's potentially something, as if it's got reserve energy that comes into use for creating a universe, that of course is actually part of itself. . . ."

"You're losing me again. How is a universe created?"

"I think that a spot in hyperspace suddenly gains a where and a when. How it's done or happens is beyond even me, so of course it's beyond everyone in the Solar System, and even if I could explain it to you, you wouldn't know how to understand it."

"Thanks for your high estimate of my intelligence. All *I* really want to know is if you can figure out how to get back to *our* Solar System."

"Certainly. I just have to tune into the pattern in hyperspace and find out where to go."

"Then you'd better do it soon. There's a bigger dragon coming."

"Perhaps," Norby said, as he backed closer to Jeff, "the little dragon's mother wants to thank us for being nice to her baby."

"Don't count on it," Jeff said, snatching up Norby. There was no use running. The dragon had long, strong legs, and wings as well. She was only as high as Jeff's chin, but she had gleaming, pointed teeth in double rows, top and bottom.

She made the same kind of sounds the little dragon had made, only much louder.

"What's she saying?" whispered Jeff.

"She says we are aliens and we might have to be taken to the Grand Dragonship unless she can teach us to talk."

"Well, what are you waiting for, Norby? Tell her you can talk."

Norby delivered a rapid patter of sounds, and the dragon responded with similar sounds.

"Jeff," Norby squawked, "let's leave right now. That foul reptile insulted me."

"What did she say?"

"She said I was simply a barrel and that I smelled of nails."

"I suppose she's right. The barrel did once—"

"Don't finish that sentence. We're going."

"No, we're not. If we dash off somewhere, we'll be lost twice as bad. Let's listen to what she has to say."

But she said nothing more. Instead she plunged toward them, plucked Norby out of Jeff's arms, and then bit Jeff on the neck. She licked her chops and wrinkled her snout as if she had tasted something bad. Then she placed Norby carefully on the ground and went back to the castle.

"Help, Norby! I've been bitten by the dragon. She's probably rabid! I've been bitten by a rabid dragon vampire!"

"Not very deeply," Norby said, examining Jeff's neck. "It's just a scratch. Barely enough to draw blood. I have a feeling there's a reason for it."

"*I* have a feeling I hurt. And *her* reason is that she wanted to taste me. Next time she'll make a meal of me. Do you want me to be eaten up by a dragon? *Think*, you dumb barrel! Get us back home. Get us anywhere! I don't care how lost we get."

My dear sir! There is no need to agitate yourself. Whoever you are, there must be communication in order for there to be a meeting of minds.

Jeff's mouth fell open. He swallowed noisily. "Norby, I just heard a voice—in my mind!"

In order to communicate with you, I had to taste your pattern since you do not understand vocal speech.

"I tell you someone's talking, Norby!"

"It's that abominably rude dragon-mother, Jeff. Do not condescend to answer her."

Just wait until I disinfect myself and my child, for we touched you, and since you are an alien you are probably full of germs.

"I am not full of germs," yelled Jeff. "You are. I'm sure I'll get tetanus from your bite. With all those teeth, you probably never use toothpaste."

No gentleman would say such a thing! I use toothpaste and

mouthwash, and so does my dear little daughter, Zargl. I think you had better leave. No respectable Jamyn would want you on this world. I will place the hyperspatial coordinates of this world in the memory bank of your storage barrel—

"Storage barrel!" cried Norby.

And I will thank you to leave.

"Do you have the coordinates, Norby?"

"Yes, but I won't use them. Not if they come from her. Not—"

"Norby, use them, or I will take you apart with my bare hands and mix you up so that you never get unmixed!"

The mother dragon appeared in the doorway of the castle, holding the baby in her arms. She made shooing gestures with her wings.

Away! Away! You crude monster!

"Come on, Norby!"

"All right, I'm trying. But I think you *are* a crude monster to make such vicious threats against me when it was only half an hour ago you were saying you loved me."

"I *do* love you, but that's beside the point. Get going!"

"Give me a chance. If you start shouting and hurrying, I'll just get mixed up."

"Must I tell you that you're always mixed up?"

"All right. I have the coordinates, and I know Earth's coordinates, and I'll concentrate on your brother. And now . . . one . . . two—I hope it works—three. . . ."

They were skimming over Manhattan Island, and Central Park was a patch of green far below.

Jeff held Norby firmly under his arm and shouted, "You're too high up, Norby. Farther down—and not too fast."

"You've got your hand over two of my eyes. All I can see are clouds and blue sky. Okay, that's better. Down we go!"

"There's a crowd in the park," Jeff said, "and they're surrounding the Central Park Precinct house. Get down so we can see what's happening."

"What if we get within blaster range?" Norby asked.

"Try not to."

"That's easy for you to say. You're not the one who's flying."

"Come on, Norby. Lower!"

The crowd was milling about as if it didn't know its own mind. They had spilled over into the traverse, along which there was no traffic.

A group of Ing's men were outside the precinct house, blasters ready. Their leader was crying out, "Disperse, you rebels, disperse, or we'll fill the park with your dead bodies."

"Do you suppose he'll really do that?" Norby asked.

"I don't know," Jeff said. "If Ing wins the day with too much bloodshed, he'll create hatred for himself, and he must know that, so I think he'd like to take over painlessly. Still, if his men get desperate—"

"Well, they're liable to, Jeff, because there's your brother and that woman policeman friend of his, and they've got personal shields on."

They could hear Fargo's voice shouting, "Forward, citizens, save our beloved island from Ing's Ignominies. Follow me!"

They didn't follow. They remained irresolute. One man shouted, "It's easy for you to say, 'Follow me'; you've got a personal shield. We don't."

"All right, then," shouted Fargo. "Watch us, and then join in. Come on, Albany. Get their blasters!"

The leading Ingman shouted, "Take them alive. Ing will pay a heavy reward for those two!"

They spread out. Fargo charged in, blocking an arm that was bringing down a blaster butt-first, and then landed a heavy blow in his assailant's solar plexus. The Ingman doubled up and lost interest in the fight for a while.

Albany Jones circled another Ingman, making little "come on" gestures with her hands. He charged, and she turned and bent, blocking the charge with her hip, seizing his wrist, and tumbling him over into another henchman. Both Ingmen went sprawling.

Norby cheered loudly. "That's it," he shouted. "Knock them all out."

"There are too many of them," said Jeff. "Fargo and Albany will be smothered after a while if the crowd doesn't help them. Norby, take me over the park. Maybe the birdwatchers are still around."

"What good will they do?"

"I want their leader, Miss Higgins. She struck me as a stalwart woman without fear, and that's the combination we want. Come on, Norby. If we can't find her, we'll have to join Fargo ourselves, and we won't be enough, either."

They were flying over Central Park in zigzags, looking for the small group with a tweed-clad woman in the lead. "What's one crazy woman going to do, Jeff?"

"I'm not sure, but I have a feeling she can help. And she's not crazy. She's enthusiastic."

"Is that they?"

"Maybe. Get down lower, and let's land on the other side of those trees. I don't want to panic them."

Jeff and Norby moved cautiously through the trees. "That's the woman," said Jeff. "Miss Higgins! Miss Higgins!"

Miss Higgins stopped and looked about. "Yes, what is it? Has anyone seen the grackle?"

"It's I, Miss Higgins."

Miss Higgins stared at Jeff for a moment. "Oh, yes," she said. "It's the young man and his little brother. We saw you at dawn, and here you are wanting to join our afternoon expedition. How enthusiastic of you."

"Not quite, Miss Higgins," said Jeff. "It's Ing and his Ingrates. They are trying to take over the park."

"*Our* park? Is that the noise we've been hearing? It scared the birds and just about ruined the afternoon watching."

"That's the noise, I'm afraid."

"Well, how dare they?"

"Perhaps you can stop them, Miss Higgins. There's a crowd of angry patriots, but they need a leader."

"Where are they?" cried Miss Higgins, waving her umbrella. "Lead me to them. Bird-watchers, wait here, and make note of any cardinals and blue jays you might see. Remember that cardinals are red and blue jays are blue!"

"We're in a hurry, Miss Higgins," said Jeff. "Would you just hold my hand?"

Miss Higgins blushed. "I suppose it would be all right. You're quite young."

Jeff seized it, pulled her closer, put his arm about her waist, and said, "All right, Norby, full power upward. You're carrying two."

Miss Higgins let out a muffled scream. "Really, young man." And then she just gasped as she rose into the air.

"Back to the precinct," shouted Jeff. "There's still fighting going on."

"It's a *beautiful* view," said Miss Higgins. "This is really the way to do bird-watching. We can follow them as they fly."

Jeff and Albany were hemmed in, and the Ingmen were very wary in their approach, but it seemed just a matter of time. A few of the Ingmen faced the crowd, holding them off with blasters.

"Get down, Norby," said Jeff. "And you, Miss Higgins, lead the crowd against those Ingmen."

"Indeed I will," said Miss Higgins. "Barbarians!"

"We're coming, Fargo," shouted Jeff.

They landed. Miss Higgins broke away quickly, and Norby rolled toward the nearest Ingman who promptly fell over him. One of Norby's arms shot outward and seized the Ingman's blaster. He flipped it to Jeff, who seized it.

Meanwhile Miss Higgins marched up to the crowd, brandishing her umbrella and shouting in a surprisingly loud voice, "Come on, you cowards. Are you going to stand there and let those villains seize your park? Central Park was made for bird-watchers and for good people, and not for villains. Save your park if you have an ounce of manhood and womanhood in you! Are you going to let me do it all alone? I'm one weak, nearly middle-aged woman, and here I go. Who'll follow me? Onward, Higgins's soldiers, marching for the right!"

She charged forward, umbrella high, and Norby suddenly shouted, "Hurrah for Miss Higgins!"

The crowd took it up, and soon there was a confused roar. "Hurrah for Miss Higgins! Hurrah for Miss Higgins!"

The mass of people moved forward, and the Ingmen instantly turned and made for the relative safety of the precinct house itself. The crowd, wild with fury, followed.

Jeff held back Norby and kept him from following. "No, no. Things are all right without us now. What we've got to do is get to Space Command. Can you do that if I give you the correct space coordinates?"

"Sure. Right through hyperspace."

"Do you have the energy?"

"You bet. I filled up on hyperspatial charge when we came through it from dragon-land."

"Good. And I must say that going through hyperspace is very pleasant. I didn't feel a thing. It was like blinking, or like a hiccup all over your insides."

"That's because I have a built-in hyperspatial shield," said Norby. "Didn't I tell you old Mac was a genius? I guess that's why I don't need a transmit. *I* am a transmit myself, and if you hold me tight, you come with me."

"How did you know I'd come with you?"

"I just guessed you would."

"What would have happened if you had guessed wrong?"

"It would have been pretty horrible for you, Jeff, but you know I'm never wrong."

"I know no such thing."

"Well, there's no use talking to you when you're *that* unreasonable. Give me the coordinates of Space Command. Okay, here we go!"

8
Showdown!

"Ouch!" said Jeff. This time he had landed on one side, still holding Norby. His right elbow hurt like mad.

"Where are we?" whispered Norby, his eyes peering from between the barrel and the hat. "Have I gotten us to the right place?"

"You have," said Jeff, sitting up with a groan.

"Never-fail Norby, they call me."

Jeff looked about and found himself in the midst of the highest officers in the Space Command, including Admiral Yobo, who looked as if he had been glaring and swearing for some time.

In back of Jeff was the open door of Space Command's transit station.

"It's working!" one of the officers cried, rushing past Jeff into the transmit.

"This boy must have come by transmit and rolled out just now," said another. "Didn't anyone see him? With this kind of security, we could expect Ing himself to appear among us."

"*I* saw him arrive," said Yobo in his rolling bass voice. "I think you'll find that however Cadet Wells arrived, the transmit is again out of order."

Again out of order, not *still*. The Admiral was careful not to describe exactly what he had seen or hint that arrival had not been by transmit. A good man, thought Jeff. Quick-thinking and on the side of all decent cadets.

"May I speak to you alone, Admiral?" Jeff asked.

Yobo stroked his chin thoughtfully, then nodded at the others—an offhand gesture that had the clear force of a command. The officers left.

"My robot—" Jeff began.

"You bought *that* robot with the money I gave you? *That* was all you could get?" said the admiral.

Norby stirred, but Jeff punched the barrel from behind to keep him quiet. "It is a very good robot," Jeff said, "with a number of good and also exasperating abilities. And he will teach me Martian Swahili in no time. He is also a clever engineer and can fix the transmit. Ing and his Ingrates have control of Manhattan and—"

"We know about that, Cadet Wells. He's issuing orders for total surrender and insists on being called 'Emperor.' My own feeling is that the transmit isn't broken, but is under control from the other end." Yobo looked calmly at Jeff. Then he said, "And what do you say about that?"

"Aren't you going to do anything?" Jeff asked.

"I'm certainly not going to surrender," Yobo said, "but I have to be careful. All of Manhattan is hostage to Ing, and other places on Earth may fall to him, too, unless—"

"Unless what, sir?"

"Unless your brother can do something. He has been my close adviser in all this. He suspected that Ing would strike at Manhattan first, and he has taken measures."

"What measures?"

"We'll have to see," said Yobo calmly. "Meanwhile, what is it you want to do? Anything besides fixing the unfixable transmit?"

"I guess my robot can't really fix the transmit if Ing's blocked it. May I consult Norby—that's my robot's name—sir?"

"Go ahead, Cadet."

Jeff bent over Norby's hat and asked in a whisper, "What now?"

Norby's answer was so soft that Jeff couldn't hear, so he

bent closer until his nose touched Norby's hat. His nose tingled and he stood up. "Ow!"

Norby's hand reached over to Jeff's leg and grabbed it hard.

I don't want the admiral to hear! I think I could gimmick a small ship (if he'll give us one) and hyperjump us to Earth.

Jeff gulped. "Norby?" he said faintly, feeling the tingle through his leg this time.

I think the dragon made you responsive to telepathy if I touch you. Get me a ship!

"Cadet Wells!" said Yobo. "Are you sane?"

"Most of the time, sir. And Norby is, too, some of the time. What we want is a small ship, just large enough to hold me and Norby."

"Why?"

"The idea is to move it past any security network Ing may have, and then fit it into his headquarters. I've been there, and I recognized it. He had it all draped in flags, but I could tell it was the main waiting room of the Old Grand Central Station. It had a museum smell about it, and I learned every inch of it when I used to visit it as a youngster. I know the transmit coordinates of the station, or at least Norby does because he memorizes transmit coordinates whenever he's been anywhere. . . ."

"Cadet, you mean well," said Yobo, "but without a transmit it will take days to get to Earth, and with a transmit you wouldn't need a ship. You don't need a ship to make a trip to Earth. I've got the fleet itself ready to do it, but Ing threatens to blow up Manhattan if I as much as move a ship."

"That's just bluff."

"You're sure of that? You'd risk Earth's most renowned relic of ancient days, its most famous center of population, on your certainty?"

"The fleet would be noticed if it made a move, but one ship—one small ship—"

"Nonsense! It would be noticed, too. You should understand the efficiency of space detection, Cadet. You've been in the academy long enough for that."

"Please, Admiral," said Jeff. "Trust me. My robot is very good with machinery, and perhaps he can speed up one of your small ships and arrange to have it deflect the spy beams and move it right into the Grand Central waiting room."

"You're suggesting an impossibility," said Yobo, "unless. . . ." He stared hard at Norby. Then he added, "Unless this—uh—barrel you clutch so tightly is by way of being a sorcerer. What about my private cruiser? Would that be small enough?"

"How small is it?"

"Small enough to hold just me, although you and your robot-barrel can squeeze in if you don't mind sleeping on the floor."

"Why would we have to sleep on the floor, sir?"

"Because you can't have my private cruiser without me on it, and I sleep in the one bed. That's the privilege of rank, Cadet."

"Take you, sir?" Jeff leaned over Norby's hat and whispered, "Can you move the admiral along with the ship and us?"

Norby squeaked, "No! Look at the size of him!"

Yobo heard that and smiled. "I'm not exactly stunted, but I am not going to sit here helpless. I've had enough of this whole thing. If you can get a ship into Grand Central Station, Cadet, I want to be with it. If anything happens to me, there are several good men—in their own estimation, if in no one else's—any one of whom could succeed me at once."

Jeff said promptly, "Norby, you can do it. Don't let me hear any negatives. Admiral, you can come, but let me be in temporary command."

"Cadet Wells," said Yobo with a grim smile, "you are more like your brother than I would have imagined. But before we make a move, you're going to tell me exactly how you expect to move the ship to Earth. Any ordinary movement and we'll be lost—and you know it."

Jeff thought awhile. "Admiral," he said, "will you give me your word that what I am about to say will be held in strictest confidence?"

"That's an impertinent request," Yobo said. "Any information you have that is of importance to system security should be delivered at once and without restrictions. What do you mean 'strictest confidence'?"

Jeff said miserably, "Well, sir, Norby can move us through hyperspace without a transmit."

"Indeed? I rather suspected you had something like that in mind, since nothing else would accomplish what you plan to do. And how does Norby bring about this impossibility?"

"I don't know. And he doesn't, either."

"After this is over, shouldn't he be taken apart so that we can find out the secret of hyperspatial travel?"

Norby squawked. "Jeff, have nothing to do with this oversize monster. He's as bad as that dragon."

"What dragon?" asked Yobo.

"Just a mythical monster, sir. But that's why I want the information held confidential. If it's found out, all the scientists would want to take him apart, and they still might not find out, and then we might not be able to put him together again, and we would end up with nothing."

"We would kill the goose that lays the golden eggs," whispered Norby angrily. "Tell him that, Jeff. Only make it a more intelligent bird."

Jeff nudged Norby into silence. "As it is, Admiral, Norby would make an important secret weapon for the Federation. He has all sorts of powers that he can handle with perfect ease—almost."

"Very well, but why aren't we taking a squadron of armed men and a battle cruiser, then?"

"Well, Admiral, Norby's powers are, for the moment, somewhat limited."

The Admiral laughed. "You mean he's a small robot and

can only handle small things."

"You are not a small thing, you overgrown human, you!" shouted Norby.

The Admiral laughed again. "I suppose I'm not. But let's go ahead, you undergrown barrel, you. I'll have my personal cruiser made ready."

An hour later they were on the cruiser, and Norby had plugged himself into the ship's engine. "I don't promise I can make this work," he grumbled. "Getting an entire ship with me through hyperspace is no small task."

"You can do it, Norby," Jeff said.

"Me? An undergrown barrel?"

"Yes, you. An ancient, intelligent, very brave, and powerful robot," said Jeff. "And if you don't, I will take out your works and fill your barrel with peanut butter—rancid peanut butter, so that the dragon-mother won't notice the nail smell anymore."

The jump through hyperspace was not *quite* perfect.

"We're not inside Grand Central." said Jeff.

"Well, there it is, right ahead," Norby said indignantly. "You have to allow for a little slippage. Ask any engineer."

"This will do fine," said the admiral. "We just require a tiny normal space correction."

Two seconds later, the Admiral's personal cruiser was hovering on an antigrav beam in the air above Ing's throne. The ship was draped in flags, and a window behind it was smashed.

"Brilliant, Admiral," said Jeff. "Brilliant."

Norby groaned. "It was my hyperspatial jump, and it's my antigrav beam. *I'm* the one who's brilliant, only I don't know how long I can hold the ship up. My insides feel as if they're caving in."

Let the Admiral get some credit, Norby, Jeff said telepathically. *Rank has its privileges.*

"Now hear this!" The Admiral's bass voice rolled out

across the vastness of the room. Ing himself, his mask still in place, was standing next to his throne looking up at the ship. He made no sound. His soldiers stood as if in a trance, stunned by the appearance of the ship.

"We have all of you under our guns," said Admiral Yobo, touching a button so that at least one gun extruded from the hull and aimed itself directly at Ing. "Put down your weapons and surrender. There will be no Solar Empire and no Emperor."

The ship settled slowly upon the throne, smashing it. Jeff heaved a sigh of relief.

Ing ran for the transmit.

"Stop him!" Jeff cried.

"We don't want to kill him," the admiral said, "or they'll make a heroic martyr out of him. Let's see, now, I might be able to destroy the transmit, but that might—"

"Let me out, Jeff," said Norby. "I'll do it."

The admiral, coming to an instant decision, touched another button, and a panel opened. "Get him, little robot!" he cried.

Norby hurtled out and aimed himself at Ing, but the transmit doors were opening and Ing was almost there.

Out of the transmit stepped Fargo, Albany, and a band of armed Manhattan policemen. "Greetings, Emperor," Fargo said with composure. "We were about to depose you, but I see from Norby here that my younger brother must have arrived with the same notion in mind. You can't beat the Wells brothers."

"Fargo," came the booming and unmistakable voice of Admiral Yobo, "what happened? Report!"

"Admiral? You're here, too? Well, it was simple. We were imprisoned here, but Albany and I got out, thanks to Norby, and after that things worked out exactly as I had hoped. The population of Manhattan was rising in revolt. It may be small, but the people of this island are very patriotic. I attacked the Central Park Precinct house and took it, aided

91

by some clever martial arts on the part of this beautiful policewoman, Albany Jones, whom I expect will be promoted as a result."

"We were also helped by a woman who said she was a bird-watcher," Albany said. "The woman, a Miss Higgins, said she didn't care what happened to the rest of the universe, but that Central Park belonged to the people. She led the crowd against Ing's Ignominies and personally incapacitated at least seven Ingrates before I lost count."

"We liberated and armed a number of policemen and then proceeded to take over other areas," Fargo continued. "At this moment any part of Manhattan not under our control is rapidly coming under it. And as for you, Ing the Inglorious, I suspect you will shortly have a large headache."

Ing had been standing in stunned and helpless silence, while his men were raising their arms in surrender. Norby, who had been circling him, now lunged for his head, which he struck with a metallic clang. Ing went down hard and, as Norby sat on him, the mask came off his face.

The admiral's voice rang out in disgust. "I might have known," he bellowed. "Ing the Intriguer is fussbudget Two Gidlow. I suspected it might be someone in Security! How else could a takeover be carried through with such precision?"

"Gidlow knew you would suspect that," Fargo said. "I think he tried to sell you the notion that I might be the traitor to turn you off the scent."

"He almost succeeded," Yobo admitted. "My apologies, Mr. Wells. I will make it up to you. The contributions of you and Cadet Jefferson Wells will not be forgotten."

"How about Norby?" shrieked Norby, pounding his feet on Gidlow-Ing's chest.

"Nor will Cadet Norby be forgotten."

"I'll be a cadet?" Norby cried out in delight.

"Honorary," the admiral said.

"Take this demon off me!" Gidlow-Ing yelled. "You can't kill me like this. I demand a fair trial."

"Let's give him a fair trial right now," Norby said.

Using his antigrav to lift him into the air, Norby clamped his legs about Ing's neck and dragged the would-be emperor to his feet. Norby swayed from side to side, forcing Ing to waltz about on his skinny, silver-covered legs.

The waiting room rocked with laughter. Even Ing's erstwhile henchmen joined in. The police photographer eagerly ran his holographic camera, filming it all in moving three-dimensional image.

"Ing's revolution is over," the admiral said. "The men of the Manhattan police force have done nobly."

"If you'll notice," Albany said, sweetly but firmly, "half the police force are women."

"True, my dear," the admiral said, and bowed to her with admiring gallantry. "And so are half of the soldiers in my Space Command. I was merely using an old-fashioned figure of speech. Which reminds me that your uniform seems to be strategically torn, and I must compliment you on *your* figure."

"Admiral," said Fargo, "it is as nothing compared with what textile dissolvers can do, but all such compliments are reserved for me."

"Then I congratulate *you*, Mr. Wells," said the admiral, "on your good taste—in cops as well as brothers."

9
Full Circle

After the revolt had been settled, there was a victory dinner in the admiral's private quarters on the great revolving wheel of Space Command.

The admiral had been given a new decoration for his broad chest. Fargo had been rewarded with a grant of money that made him thoroughly safe from bankruptcy. Albany, who sat close beside him—very close—had been promoted to Police Lieutenant Jones. And Jeff had been given a scholarship and a commendation, too, so that he could continue his studies as a Space Cadet.

Norby sat in the seat next to Jeff's, with a large portfolio under his arm. Within the portfolio was the official piece of pseudo-parchment that proclaimed to "all and sundry to whom this citation shall come to notice" that Norby Wells was hereby appointed to the rank of Honorary Cadet in the Space Command "with all the privileges and honors inseparable from that position." Norby had not yet found out what those privileges and honors were, but he was still asking.

Jeff noted with satisfaction, for he was still a growing boy, that the food at the admiral's table was considerably better than the food at the cadets' table. Norby had an extension cord leading into the nearest electric plug, and he was gorging himself to repletion, though, as he remarked later, the admiral's electricity tasted no better than anyone else's.

"I guess the kitchen computer is working now, eh, Admiral?" Jeff said.

"Perfectly," said the Admiral with great satisfaction.

"You can thank Norby for that," Jeff said. "He's very good with computers."

"When I fix them," Norby said, "they work like poetry in motion."

"Good," said the admiral. "But, Fargo, what was that remark you made to your brother the day he ruined the computer—TGAF?"

"It stood for 'The Game's A-Foot.' It was my way of telling him that he and I were going to try to find Ing. I didn't know he was right there with you. One thing, though, Admiral. . . ."

"Yes?"

"Confining Ing to an asteroid prison doesn't seem enough. Security is notoriously lax in the asteroids, and he may get out."

"What if he does?" the admiral said indifferently. "Everyone's laughing at him. The quickness with which his attempted revolt collapsed and the holographic images of his final dance with Norby on top of him have reduced him to a figure of fun. The film has been shown throughout the Solar System. He could do nothing at all now, even if he were released."

"I don't know about that," Jeff said darkly.

A junior officer, looking uneasy, rushed into the room. "Admiral!"

"Yes, Ensign?"

"The main computer of Space Command has just started reciting poetry. All the messages come out in verse, including the recipes from your private kitchen computer, which is now too addled to get the robot cooks to perform properly."

The admiral rose from his chair. Putting his napkin gently beside his place, he asked, "*My* kitchen computer?"

"Yes, sir. The remainder of this meal will be delayed."

The admiral roared, "Norby!"

There was no response.

"Norby!" Jeff shouted, banging on Norby's head.

Norby said in a low, snuffling voice, "I told the computers to work like poetry in motion. Maybe they took me literally.

Computers are *very* stupid."

The admiral roared, "I demand that this barrel—"

"*Cadet* barrel," said Norby in a whisper.

"—be thrown in irons."

"Please, Admiral," said Jeff, "he'll fix it in a jiffy."

"I give him fifteen minutes."

"Norby, get rid of the extension and get to work."

"Oh, all right, but it's the fault of the computers."

"And of a very mixed-up robot," Jeff said. He looked up defiantly at the rest of the company. "But *my* very mixed-up robot, and no one else can touch him. Not even you, Admiral."